ENTHRALLED

BOOK FIVE IN THE ROGUES SERIES

Enthralled

A kidnapper on the loose, and a brother hell bent on revenge

Fifty million dollars. That's how much my sister's freedom cost. She's moved on. I haven't. I think about the horror of her kidnapping *every day.* Every hour. Every goddamn second.

Someone has to pay.

Yet despite my relentless searching, each road leads to a dead end. Until a chance meeting with my secret high school crush changes everything.

She promises answers where I only have questions. She vows to support me on my quest for justice.

Except I'm on a path to self-destruction, and if she's not careful, I'll take her down with me.

A note to the reader

Dear Reader,

Oh my goodness! It's here. Elliot Bancroft finally gets his place in the sun—and boy he takes advantage of every single second.

Out of all the ROGUES series books, Enthralled is the one that I've had most of the messages and emails about and I am so excited that I can finally release the fifth, and penultimate, book in the series.

I'm proud of every single novel I write, and I adore the ROGUES so much, but Elliot is special. I'll always have a soft spot for him, in a similar way I adore Cash Gallagher from my Winning Ace series. There are certain characters that, as the author, I get all the feels for as they slowly reveal their story to me, and Elliot is one of those characters. I hope you adore him as much as I do.

And Sage... wow. What can I say about her? She is fierce, has strength in spades, and is pretty bad ass. But oh my is she a perfect match for Elliot, just as he is for her. I love, love, love these two together.

I hope you enjoy reading Elliot and Sage's story. Do message me with your thoughts after you've finished reading, or join my Facebook reader group Tracie's Racy Aces, and take part in the discussion over there.

In the meantime, dive in. Enjoy every moment. Elliot and Sage can't wait for you to join them.

Happy reading.

Love,
Tracie

Books by Tracie Delaney

BILLIONAIRE ROMANCE

The ROGUES Series

The Irresistibly Mine Series

The Kincaid Billionaire Series

PROTECTOR/MILITARY ROMANCE

The Intrepid Bodyguard Series

SPORTS ROMANCE

The Winning Ace Series

The Full Velocity Series

CONTEMPORARY ROMANCE

The Brook Brothers Series

BOXSETS

Winning Ace

Brook Brothers

Full Velocity

ROGUES Books 1-3

Chapter One

ELLIOT

THE CRUSHING PAIN AT MY TEMPLE CAME IN ferocious waves. I pinched the bridge of my nose and held my breath in an attempt to stem the hideous throbbing. Filan, my driver, took a corner a bit too fast, and I hissed.

"Slow the fuck down, will you? I'd like to get home in one piece."

He shot me an apologetic smile in the rearview mirror, unfazed by my grouchiness. Filan, a wily old Irish guy, had been with me for years, and a snide comment or barbed response didn't bother him in the slightest.

Lucky for me.

Especially these days, given my moods favored the dark side. The only person in the world who seemed able to force a genuine smile from me anymore was my nephew, Ethan. Nine weeks ago—the day he was born—he stole my heart, and the little fucker refused to give it back.

Thinking about Ethan turned my thoughts to my sister, Athena. Four years had gone by since someone had snatched her off the streets and held her captive until a huge ransom changed hands. Following her release, she'd dealt with it like the remarkable woman she was. As for me, I simmered, like a volcano threatening to erupt and wipe out everything in its path. Her kidnapping had rocked the foundation beneath my feet, and with each passing year, the ground thinned to a danger point, a massive eruption creeping ever closer as each lead led to a dead end.

Sometimes I felt as if I were losing my mind. And without an outlet to channel the ever-present negative energy, I feared losing control. I despised the man I'd become. Vengeful, bitter, a shadow of the easy-going, care-free man of my youth. Yet no matter how I strived to find him, he was lost to me.

I still clung enough to the shreds of my sanity to know this desire to find the perpetrator had strayed dangerously into obsessive territory. It *consumed* me. It *devoured* me. It monopolized my every waking moment, and my anger built with each passing day.

In the beginning, I'd turned to Ryker. My best friend. My brother-in-law, and together, we'd explored every lead, followed each clue. But these days he was far too preoccupied with Athena and his son to pay heed to my fixation on Athena's abductor. I didn't begrudge him a single second of happiness. Fuck knows, he'd waited long enough for it. But without his solid presence and cool head to ground me, I was terrified that I'd give in to the rage that had devoured me for four years.

Their blissful happiness sat in stark contrast to my lone-liness. I felt disconnected, cast adrift, distant from everything that I once held so dear. I resented that they'd somehow managed to put that horrifying time behind them while I still lived it every single day. I couldn't let go. I'd made a promise to Mom and to Athena long ago that I'd protect her.

And I'd failed.

My phone vibrated against my chest, and I slipped it from the inside pocket of my suit jacket. A text from Ryker. Following up, no doubt, on the three voicemails he'd left asking me to call him the second I arrived back in the country. Suffice to say I hadn't returned a single one. Tired and cranky after the flight—not to mention dangerously frustrated given the trip had resulted in another fucking dead end—all I craved was a glass of scotch and Brie's warm body.

I opened the text.

The Saunders deal is off.
Call me the second you land.
We need to talk.

I cursed. Filan glanced in the mirror for a moment before returning his attention to the road the second he met my fiery gaze, no doubt.

Fucking hell!

A one hundred million dollar deal and a year of my life down the fucking drain. And worst of all, it wasn't a surprise. I'd fucked up. Taken my eye off the ball to fly off to Switzerland on another pointless wild goose chase. Saunders wouldn't forget this easily. Corpses of businesses he'd destroyed littered the streets of Manhattan. I'd have to grovel and hope I could salvage something.

Inhaling a deep breath through my nose, I slowly blew it out, repeating the action several times. Tomorrow, after a good night's sleep, I'd call him, talk to him, promise him that, from now on, he'd have my full attention until the ink dried on the mutually beneficial contract. I owed him that much. Fuck, I owed ROGUES that and so much more.

I switched off my phone and returned it to my pocket, shifting my attention to Brie. Maybe we should take a trip. We'd grown further and further apart these past few months, and I took the lion's share of the blame for creating this atmosphere between us. She wasn't expecting me back for another couple of days, and I purposely hadn't called her to let her know I'd decided to come home early. I wanted to surprise her. Tell her I'd missed her, and that was why I'd cut the trip short.

It wasn't the reason. I hadn't missed her at all, but what she didn't know wouldn't hurt her. In truth, I hadn't thought about her once since I boarded my plane three days ago. Whenever I was following a lead, it drained all my energy, used up every inch of headspace.

Hence the fucked-up Saunders deal.

Filan stopped the car on the street outside the house I shared with my girlfriend. For years after my company, ROGUES, made it into the big leagues, I lived with my parents and my sister in a home I bought for them. Even when I started dating Brie, I saw no reason to move out. I enjoyed living with Mom and Dad. They were more like friends than parents. But then Athena hooked up with Ryker, and Brie began applying pressure, asking the dreaded "Where is this going?" question. I didn't even remember asking her to move in with me, too preoccupied with all the other shit demanding my attention. Before I knew it, I'd bought a six-bed nine-bath house in Greenwich Village, mainly because it was within easy commuting distance from the ROGUES offices, and Brie and I moved in.

Six bedrooms for just the two of us. The irony wasn't

lost on me. We didn't even own a dog or a cat. But Brie had fallen in love with the place and even hinted at those bedrooms not remaining empty for long.

Seriously, that conversation hadn't given me chills; it'd given me fucking frostbite.

I wanted to be a father. Someday. Just not now.

"Thanks for the puke-inducing ride, Filan," I said, accompanying my comment with a forced grin.

"We aim to please," Filan replied. "You need anything else?"

I shook my head. "See you in the morning. Can you pick me up at seven? I want to get into the office early."

"I'll be here."

He walked my suitcase over to the front door, even though I'd told him on several previous occasions not to bother. When he continued to ignore me, I stopped correcting him, figuring he liked to do it. I watched the car drive away, then entered the house.

"Brie?" I called out. Not that I expected her to hear me, especially if she was on one of the upper levels, but I did it anyway. Sure enough, she didn't reply. I left my case by the front door and wandered through the first floor, poking my head into the living room, the library, and then the kitchen, all her usual haunts. All empty.

Figuring she must be out, I trudged upstairs to our bedroom on the third floor. A hot shower and a bite to eat and I'd be as good as new.

Yeah, sure.

More like vaguely passable for a human being.

Maybe.

I wished this shit would just fuck off, but long ago, I'd accepted it would only after I found the man responsible for taking Athena—and that seemed further away than ever.

I turned the door handle to our bedroom and pushed it open.

It took me a few seconds of jaw-dropping staring to figure out what the fuck was going on. Brie, my *fucking girlfriend*, was on all fours on top of our bed, and a guy kneeled behind her, furiously pounding into her.

A white-hot rage surged within me, and I launched.

Brie's piercing screams reached me through a dense fog. I slumped against the wall, staring at the bloody, crumpled heap of the stranger groaning, his fingers clawing at the carpet as he crawled. No fucking idea where he thought he was crawling to.

"What have you done?" Brie screeched.

The sound of my own ragged breathing roared in my ears, and my chest heaved. I fought to catch my breath, blinking as I stared at Brie crouched next to the stranger.

"I'm calling the police," she cried, sprinting for her phone sitting on top of the nightstand.

I flexed my bloodied knuckles, the skin pulling painfully tight. My knees went from underneath me, and I slid down the wall, landing with a thud. I lifted my eyes, my gaze falling on Brie just standing there, pale-faced, her hand covering her mouth, her horrified expression locked on me. She'd put on a silk robe, one I'd bought for her for Christmas eleven days earlier.

I waited for betrayal to hit me, but it never came. I felt *nothing*. Her indiscretion meant little more than a shrug of my shoulders. Realization rained down that our relationship had transformed into a habit, a bad habit that I should have broken a long time ago.

"You could have killed him."

I found my voice, the shock at the loss of control receding. I'd feel it later, but right now, numbness prevailed, along with a desire to lash out with words instead of fists.

"Nah." I pushed as much disdain into my expression as I could. "He's not worth it. And neither are you."

Her face crumpled, but she arranged it pretty damn fast into a hard glare. "What did you expect, Elliot? You're barely here, and when you are, your mind is elsewhere. Face it, we've been having problems for ages."

"I've had the same thought myself, Brie," I bit out. "The difference between us is that I chose not to solve my problems by fucking other women, despite having more opportunities than I care to count. Call me old-fashioned, but integrity and faithfulness are important to me. It's a shame they're not values that you hold dear." I sneered at her. "I must remember to book an STI test. Who knows how many dicks your pussy has entertained each time I've gone away?"

"You bastard," she hissed.

I shrugged. "At least I'm not a fucking whore."

I cringed even as I said those words, but I couldn't stop them. Maybe her infidelity bothered me more than I originally thought. Or maybe it had more to do with the fact my ego had taken a battering at a time I needed a boost.

She burst into tears. The jerkoff she'd been fucking made a move to comfort her. I stopped him in his tracks with a single look, and he retreated, slinking away into one corner of the room.

"I don't even know who you are any more, Elliot," she sobbed. "I was lonely. All I wanted was some attention. To feel attractive, desired. Visible."

Several firm raps on the door saved me from answering. I

was done talking to her. I got to my feet and trudged downstairs to let the police in. Two cops stood on the doorstep. I didn't even glance at them, just left the door wide open and spun on my heel.

A vaguely familiar voice made me pull up fast.

"Elliot Bancroft. What trouble have you gotten yourself into now?"

Chapter Two

SAGE

A STIFF WIND COULD'VE KNOCKED ME OVER, SUCH was my amazement when Elliot Bancroft opened the door to the house despatch had sent us to following a call about an alleged assault. One quick glance told me he was the assailant rather than the victim. The telltale signs of bruised and grazed knuckles, and not a single scratch on his handsome face, was damning evidence.

Like a movie from the twenties whose reel played on double-time, my last year of high school raced before me. I'd been the shy, awkward girl with braces, lank, greasy hair, and a body thin as a rake who'd blended into the background. Elliot, on the other hand, had been the most popular guy in school. Tall, ridiculously good-looking with striking amber eyes, thick dark hair, and a muscular physique, even then. Now... it was safe to say that time had only increased his attractiveness.

And just like all those years before, he hadn't given me a second glance, just opened the door, turned his back, and walked away. When I called out to him, he froze on the spot, then slowly pivoted around.

His eyes narrowed as he peered at me. "Do I know you?"

I suppressed a sigh. At least I thought I had, but judging by Elliot's frown, I hadn't totally succeeded. *Still the invisible girl, Sage.* At least I no longer wore braces, my hair wasn't greasy, and I'd developed curves. Not that they were easily seen under a police uniform and a thick utility belt. None of those things mattered to Elliot, though. I scanned around the large entranceway. He'd obviously done well for himself. Very well. A house this size, in this location, had to run into tens of millions of dollars. His obvious wealth didn't surprise me. He, along with his best friend, Ryker Stone, always had that edge. The one that screamed victory was right around the corner, theirs for the taking.

I stepped inside and gestured to Bryce, my partner, to follow me. "Sage Abbott," I said. "We went to high school together."

Two dark eyebrows flew toward his hairline, creasing his forehead. "Sage? Wow."

His eyes roved over my face. Weirdly, I took no comfort from the fact they didn't slide any lower.

"God, I hardly recognize you."

"Fifteen years is a long time." I cleared my throat. "We got a call about an alleged assault. What's going on?"

Right at that moment, a tall, willowy woman made her way downstairs followed by the clear victim in this altercation. A quick scan of his injuries and the way he held himself, I'd guess a broken nose, possibly a broken jaw, and at least a few cracked ribs.

"I can tell you," the woman said, jabbing a finger in Elliot's direction. "He went crazy."

"Yeah, that'll happen, Brie, when a man comes home to find another guy balls deep inside his woman."

Bryce made a snuffling noise that I knew all too well was a suppressed laugh. I shot him a glare. "Why don't you call an ambulance for this gentleman and take the two of them into that room," I pointed at what appeared to be a living area, "and I'll have a chat separately with Mr. Bancroft."

I waited until Bryce closed the door, blocking off our view, then returned my attention to Elliot. I gestured with my hand, and he led me through to an enormous, sleek kitchen, all granite and stainless steel, with floor-to-ceiling windows that looked out onto the inky blackness.

"Can I get you anything to drink?" Elliot asked politely, but behind the manners, his eyes were flat, his tone despondent. Despite that, he was even more attractive than he had been at school. Close-cut dark hair, a well-trimmed beard that didn't detract from a strong jaw, and those amber irises that'd bewitched more than half the girls in our senior class. Plus, he'd filled out, his teenage body morphing into broad shoulders, a tapered waist, and just the way he held his body and how easily he moved about the space told me he took care of himself physically.

I pushed all inappropriate thoughts to the back of my mind, reminded myself I was on duty and had a job to do, and reached into my pocket for a notebook and pen. "Why don't you tell me what happened."

Elliot took a seat at the island in the center of the kitchen. I remained standing. His shoulders bowed, and a deep sigh pulled from his chest.

"There isn't a lot to tell. I came home from a... a business trip and walked in on her and him fucking." He hitched up his right shoulder. "I lost my temper and punched him. I'm not contesting any of it."

"Where did your trip take you?" I asked.

"What's that got to do with anything?" he snapped, then he scraped a hand down his face. "Sorry, that was uncalled for. I flew in this afternoon from Switzerland."

"Lucky you," I muttered to myself. I'd never left the continental US, and on my salary, and with mounting debts from taking care of my mom and my sister, I doubted I ever would.

"You think?" he asked, his fingers almost white where he gripped the granite countertop.

Mortified that he'd heard me, I glanced at my notebook, bought myself a few seconds, then lifted my chin. "Do you want me to have the medic examine you, too?" I asked. When he frowned, I pointed to his hands. "They look sore."

"Not as sore as that fucker's face," he deadpanned.

"You're not helping your case here," I advised. "This works in my favor, but maybe you should call a lawyer and ask them to meet us down at the station."

"Why pay a lawyer when I've admitted everything?" Elliot sighed. "Just book me, and then we can both get on with our lives."

Bryce's footsteps squeaked on the tiled floor, and seconds later he poked his head into the kitchen and cocked his head, beckoning me to follow him. "A word."

"Wait here," I said to Elliot, not that I thought for one second that he'd make a run for it. I joined Bryce in the entranceway.

"He wants to press charges," Bryce said.

I nodded. I'd expected he would. "He's admitted to assault," I said, jerking my head back to denote Elliot. "I'll cuff and Miranda him. Tell them to follow us down once the paramedics have given the vic the all-clear. We'll need to take their formal statements."

"Will do."

I returned to the kitchen, my handcuffs already unhooked from my belt. Elliot rose as I entered and turned around, his hands clasped behind his back. I clicked the cuffs into place and led him out front. We passed by his girlfriend and the other man on the way. Elliot skidded to a halt, his amber eyes burning a hole in his girlfriend's face as he glared at her. "Don't be here when I get back, Brie."

"This is my home, too, Elliot," she cried.

"No, darling," he drawled. "My name is on the deeds. You got to stay here as long as your legs opened only for me. Suffice to say you fucked that one up big-time."

I pushed him out the door before any more fists went flying. We got him in the squad car, and Bryce drove us to the station. We traveled down roads smattered with a dusting of snow, and I snatched an occasional sneak peek at Elliot. He stared out the window, his expression bleak and filled with a sadness that appeared to go far deeper than what happened tonight.

An urge to know more stole over me, but at the same time, warning lights flashed in front of my eyes. In the fourteen years I'd spent working for the New York Police Department, I'd seen enough men who screamed *danger* to have me racing in the opposite direction at the mere sniff of one. And menace radiated off Elliot Bancroft.

Gone was the happy-go-lucky boy who'd had girls falling at his feet. In his place was a man with a cruel streak that he somehow blended with vulnerability.

A perilous combination, and one I'd do well to avoid at all costs.

So why didn't I want to?

Chapter Three

ELLIOT

SAGE ABBOTT. THE VERY LAST PERSON I'D expected to turn up at my door, much less haul me off to the local precinct. And what the hell was she doing patrolling the streets weighed down with twenty pounds of gear? In high school, she'd had ambitions to go to college and study architecture. She should be designing the buildings of the future, not mixing it up with the worst of society.

Of which I was now a fully paid-up member.

And boy, had she changed. Then again, hadn't we all? She'd been my secret crush during our senior year. Not that I'd have ever admitted it to anyone, not even Ryker. Back then, I'd encapsulated the standing of 'most popular boy,' attracting the cheerleader crowd. Sage had blended into the background, not even worthy of attention from the mean girls. I'd noticed her, though. She'd always had a quiet quality. On the rare times our eyes had met in the halls as we dashed between classes, a tingle had run from the top of my head to the tips of my toes. There was just something about her, an intangible appeal that was impossible to isolate. Fifteen years later, she still had it—supercharged.

I kept sneaking glances at her when she wasn't looking, a heat in my groin area alerting me to a schoolboy attraction that hadn't lessened over time. And now that Brie and I were no more, I had no need to feel guilty. Nor did I have to feel that I was cheating on Brie for finding myself attracted to another woman.

Instead, *she'd* been the one to cheat on *me*.

I waited for the sense of loss to overwhelm me, but it never came. Brie was right, we had been drifting apart for ages, and I had neglected her and our relationship. Even when I fucked her, it felt more like slipping into a comfortable pair of shoes than a frantic need to get inside her panties, and while all relationships mellowed over time, four years was far too soon to slot ourselves into the functional 'twice-a-week screw' category.

If I was truly honest with myself, the beating I'd given that bastard had more to do with my bruised ego than Brie cheating on me. I should feel anger, betrayal. Instead, I felt a sense of relief that I could give all my spare time to finding Athena's abductor, and start to pay ROGUES some much-needed attention, without having to juggle the demands of a girlfriend as well.

And even as that thought filled my mind, I realized her adultery had done me a favor. Deep down, I'd been searching for a way to break things off without crushing her, and now I didn't have to bother worrying about her feelings. I came out of this the injured party, with Brie as the villain. It wasn't how I would have chosen to end a four-year relationship, but I wasn't sorry that it had.

Sage's warm hand on my elbow as she propelled me into

the police station sent a long-forgotten shiver of pleasure shooting up my spine. Maybe after all this shit was done with, I should ask her out on a date. I could even couch it as a catch-up between old friends. Not that we'd ever been friends, at least not in the true sense of the word. A minor point I wouldn't let stop me if I chose to follow up.

Sage insisted I call a lawyer for my protection, and I reluctantly agreed. As it turned out, her advice did me a solid. The custody sergeant charged me with third-degree assault, a misdemeanor offense. A few hours later I stood in front of the judge, pleaded guilty, and received a hefty fine. My lawyer handled the paperwork, and in no time, I found myself standing on the concrete steps outside the courthouse. I shook my lawyer's hand and thanked him. In hindsight, I should have asked him for a ride home, or at least called a cab. Instead, I did something really stupid. I called Ryker.

He arrived within fifteen minutes. His scowl was so deep, all the Botox in the world wouldn't fix him. I climbed in the passenger seat, and although I deserved a lecture, I wasn't in the mood.

"Don't say a word, Ryker. Just take me home."

Very few things surprised me these days—seeing Sage Abbott tonight was an exception—but Ryker remaining tight-lipped as he drove away certainly achieved that. I'd expected him to go to town on my ass. For the lost Saunders deal, for beating up that jerkoff who'd fucked Brie, for getting arrested. For not calling him when I landed, as he'd expressly requested—no, demanded.

I stared out the window, running the events of the evening over in my mind, and I must have been so lost inside my thoughts that I only realized Ryker hadn't driven me home when he pulled up in one of his personalized parking spaces beneath his apartment building.

I shot him a glare. "What are we doing here?"

Refusing to answer, he unclipped his seat belt and climbed out, then strode over to the private elevator that would take him straight up to the penthouse. With a sigh, I followed him, only just making it before the doors closed. Bastard wasn't even going to hold the doors open for me.

As it whisked us to the top floor, Ryker set his ice-blue eyes on me. "You're staying here tonight. Athena has made up a bed for you."

"I'm not a fucking charity case," I grumbled. "I have a perfectly good house with six functioning bedrooms." Make that five. I'd already decided to burn everything in the one where Brie had fucked her lover. Didn't need those visuals, thanks very much.

"I think it's best if you and Brie keep away from each other tonight, don't you?"

"Tonight? Try forever," I muttered.

Ryker sighed, raking a hand through his dark hair. It stuck up at all angles.

"You need a haircut," I observed.

His lips quirked, but the full smirk never arrived. "She called me, Elliot. Said you'd gone fucking crazy. That you nearly killed the guy."

Ah, so Ryker already knew what had happened—or at least Brie's version of events. No wonder he hadn't asked me what the fuck I was doing at the courthouse.

"She's exaggerating. I didn't almost kill him. Neither of them is worth doing a stretch for. Believe me."

The elevator glided to a stop, and the doors smoothly opened. Ryker strode through the foyer and into the living area with me dragging my ass behind him. He went straight over to Athena and kissed her, then shrugged off his coat and tossed it over the back of one of the chairs at the breakfast bar. Athena turned her attention to me, and I smirked out an apology.

"Sorry to barge in like this, sis."

"Oh, Elliot." She came over and wrapped me in a warm hug. "Do you want something to eat or drink?"

"Not hungry, but I wouldn't say no to a scotch."

She kissed my cheek. "Coming right up."

I trailed my fingers over the back of the couch. "Can I go see my little guy? I won't wake him. Promise."

"No," Ryker snapped. "Sit your ass down, Elliot. We need to talk."

"Ryker," Athena scolded, handing me my drink. "Leave him be for tonight. It's one in the morning. It can wait."

"No, it can't."

He took a seat in a squishy chair and crossed his ankle over the opposite knee, the epitome of relaxed, in direct contrast to his snippy attitude and pissed-off expression.

I knocked back half the scotch, welcoming the burn in my throat. "If you're going to lecture me about what happened, save it. I admit I might've gone a tad too far, but come on. He was fucking my girlfriend. You'd have done the same."

"I'm not talking about Brie. And you're right. I would have. Probably a lot worse. I'm talking about you, Elliot." He jabbed his finger in my direction as if to stress his point.

I sat across from him and swirled my scotch. "What about me?"

"You're losing it. Your edge has gone. You're distracted,

disorganized, and, honestly, downright useless when it comes to ROGUES."

"Whoa. Kick a man while he's down, why don't you?"

He shook his head and leaned forward, propping his elbows on his knees. "You know as well as I do that you're riding a slippery slope. You want to press the self-destruct button? Then there's nothing I can do to stop you. You're a grown-assed man who can make his own decisions. But if you think me or any of the other guys are letting you take ROGUES down with you, forget it."

Athena moved behind Ryker and rested a hand on his shoulder while I sat there, dumbfounded.

"Go easy, yeah?" she murmured.

I pinched the bridge of my nose. "I'm at fault for Saunders pulling out. I admit it. I'll call him in the morning and square things. The deal isn't lost."

"Yes, it is," Ryker bit out. "I've already tried to talk to him, but it's too late. He told me this latest slipup of yours is the last in a long line. He's cut you all the slack you're getting, and now he's cutting us loose." Ryker wearily swiped a hand down his face. "Saunders has a lot of connections, Elliot. If he decides to share his experience with them, we could find ourselves on a floating ice shelf. Cast adrift, business wise."

"Fuck." I rubbed my forehead. "I will call him and apologize. Even if the deal is dead in the water, a bit of groveling can still go a long way."

Ryker nodded crisply. "I think that's the least you can do."

I let my head flop back against the couch and closed my eyes, hoping that was the end of the lecture. But, no, Ryker wasn't anywhere close to being done.

"I take it this latest jaunt led to another brick wall?"

I opened my heavy lids to acknowledge him. "Yup."

"For fuck's sake, Elliot. Let it go, man. It's been four years and—"

I cut him off with a flick of my wrist. "Stop. You're wasting your breath. I don't want to hear it. You might've given up, but I haven't. And I never will. I mean..." I laughed. "She's *your* wife. The mother of *your* son. You should care, yet it's me out there day after day searching for the bastard who—"

"Enough!" Athena yelled. "For Christ's sake, that's enough!" She threw her hands in the air. "I get it, Elliot. I know how terrified you were." She flashed her eyes in Ryker's direction. "How terrified you both were that something dreadful would happen. But I survived. I got over it, so did Ryker. Mom, Dad, we all found a way past this. But you..." She sighed heavily. "You're fixated, Elliot, and it's wrecking your life. Don't you see? He's winning, because *you're* letting him win. He kidnapped me, but you're the one trapped."

Fury propelled me to my feet. "It was my job to protect you," I roared. "It was *my* job, and I failed. I should have realized the dangers. Wealth causes all kinds of crazy people to surface, and yet I left you exposed." I raked both hands through my hair, leaving them there. "When I realized you were gone, I was petrified he'd kill you. That I'd lose you forever, and it'd all be my fault." I tugged on the roots, the pain allowing a distraction from the chaotic storm of emotions swirling through me. "When you walked through that door, relatively unscathed, I made a promise, Athena. A promise I *will not* break, no matter how many years pass. I *will* see that bastard brought to justice for what he did. I will live to see him rot in prison, or so help me God, I'll die trying."

My chest rose and fell, and I spun away, buying breathing space to get myself under control. A shuffle sounded behind me, and Athena appeared on my left. She slipped an arm around my waist and rested her head on my shoulder.

"I love you, Elliot, and I'm so lucky to have you as my brother. But I don't want this life for you. Drop it, please. I'm begging you."

I kissed the top of her head. "I love you to the moon and back, sis. Always have. And if I had it in me to forget about this, believe me, I would. In a heartbeat." I clenched my fist and punched at the space over my heart. "But in here, Athena. In here, I can't. I'm not an idiot, whatever he might think." I jerked my chin at Ryker and offered a faint smile, one meant to soften the harsh edges of my rant. He didn't respond in kind, his expression closed off. I metaphorically shrugged and returned my attention to Athena. "I'm aware that the more time that passes, the chances of finding out who took you get slimmer and slimmer. But I have to try. Until every single lead dries up, I can't stop looking."

Athena side-eyed Ryker, and her shoulders lifted as she breathed in. "I did my best."

Ryker nodded, and something in his body language made me pause and take notice. A sliver of ice trickled down my spine.

"What's going on?" I asked, unsure whether I wanted to hear the answer.

Ryker set his eyes on me, his gaze unwavering. "You're out, Elliot. You and ROGUES are finished."

Chapter Four

ELLIOT

KNEE-DEEP IN SILENCE, IT TOOK ME A FEW SECONDS to recover my voice. Even then, my jaw flapped about as if his words alone had broken it, and when I spoke, the sound came out rasping and hoarse.

"What did you say?"

Athena's stricken expression as she plucked repeatedly at the hem of her shirt gave me all the information I needed. It was clear she and Ryker had spoken about this ahead of time. And while it shouldn't sting that they'd talked behind my back, it did. Worse than sting. It hurt like a motherfucker.

Ryker's eyes bored into mine, and a tic vibrated in his cheek. "We can't carry on like this, Elliot. You think I want to do this? No, I fucking don't. You're my best friend. My brother-in-law, for Christ's sake, but I have to think of ROGUES. All our futures depend on it. Not just yours and mine, but Garen's, Upton's, Oliver's, and Sebastian's. Each of them deserves the very best we can give, and right now, your best falls far short of what's required."

"You can't kick me out of my own company," I scoffed.

"Alone, no, you're right. I can't. It takes a majority vote of the board. And if you want to take it that far, that's up to you, but you should know that the vote will go against you. If humiliation is what you're interested in, then fine. I'll call an emergency board meeting for tomorrow rather than wait until our scheduled meeting next Friday."

As the reality of his words sank in, my blood chilled, its icy voyage through my veins bringing my thoughts to a screeching halt. My hands fisted without my permission. I swung my gaze around the pristine living room with its priceless pieces of art adorning the walls and expensive ornaments dotted about, and my vision painted red. I imagined clawing my fingernails through the canvas of Ryker's favorite Renoir, or sweeping my arm along the sideboard and sending everything smashing to the floor.

I did none of those things. Instead, I held myself together with shallow breaths and the knowledge that my relationship with my sister and my best friend hinged on what I said or did next.

"You've spoken to them already."

A statement, not a question. Ryker responded anyway with a curt nod.

"I'm out for good?" Without ROGUES I'd be rudderless, cast adrift from the only thing that kept me sane, even if I was fucking everything up left, right, and center.

"No." Ryker rose to his feet. He placed a hand on my shoulder and squeezed. "I want you back, Elliot. But not this version of you. I miss my friend desperately. We all miss you. But you can't go on like this. Take a sabbatical. Travel the world. Get your head on straight, and once you're ready, we'll welcome you back with our arms wide open and the biggest smiles on our faces."

I shot another glance at Athena. Tears glistened in her eyes, devastation curving her shoulders, and inside, something in me broke. I held out my arms, and she ran into them, hugging me so tightly I could barely breathe. I kissed the top of her head, then released her.

"I've heard everything you've both said." I cut my gaze to Ryker. "I'm sorry that I let you down, that I haven't given ROGUES my best. And as much as it pains me to say it, if I stood where you are right now, I'd do exactly the same." I swept a hand over my face, exhaustion weighing me down. "Now can I go and see my nephew?"

Athena pressed her palm to my cheek, her smile tinged with sadness. "Yes, but if you wake him, you're staying up all night getting him back to sleep."

I laughed, and for the first time in a very long time, it didn't feel forced. "Deal."

Ethan's baby smell hit me the second I opened the door to his nursery. Decked out in blues and yellows, the room cocooned me in a warmth that I never wanted to leave. I tiptoed to his crib and peered over the top. His chubby arms were up by his ears, his legs spread wide. Ever so gently, Athena's warning ringing in my ears, I stroked the mop of dark hair on top of his head.

"What am I gonna do, little bud?"

I pulled over the rocking chair from the corner of the room and sat in it, listening to Ethan's breathing. I must have fallen asleep because the next thing I remembered was waking up, and when I checked my watch, I saw it was three o'clock in the morning. With a final peek at Ethan, I wearily got to my feet, trudged into the guest room, and collapsed facedown onto the bed.

The sound of a crying baby woke me. I squinted at the clock and groaned. With my eyelids glued together, I stumbled to the bathroom. I quickly showered and shaved—God bless Athena and her fully stocked guest baths—and dressed in the same clothes as last night, sent a text to Filan telling him I no longer needed him to pick me up at home this morning, and headed downstairs. I found my sister pacing the kitchen with an inconsolable Ethan. She shot me a desperate smile, then thrust him into my arms.

"Here, Uncle Elliot. You try to soothe him. I'll put a pot of coffee on." She yawned. "Six-thirty. Gah! Evidently, we still haven't gotten this sleep thing buttoned down."

I grinned and hoisted him up onto my shoulder, my hand beneath his butt, and I rubbed his back and hummed to him. A few minutes later, he stopped crying and promptly fell asleep.

"Right, that's it," Athena said, setting a steaming cup of coffee on the counter. "You have a new job. You start today."

"Not a chance." I shook my head to reiterate the point. "I might be unemployed, but nanny is not going on my résumé."

I set Ethan down in his bassinet and pulled out a chair at the breakfast bar. Athena joined me, peering at me over the top of her cup.

"How are you doing after what happened last night? No bullshit."

Sighing, I lowered my chin to my chest. "I'm pissed. At Ryker. At the ROGUES guys for talking about me behind my back. At you, even. But more than all of that, I'm pissed at myself."

"Hmm." She scratched her cheek. "Odd that you didn't add Brie to that list of people who've pissed you off."

My gaze shifted from my sister to the clouds rolling in. Seconds later, rain pelted the glass. I stared at the rivulets of water running down the panes and gave her comment serious consideration. And the answer I came up with aligned precisely with the answer I'd gotten last night.

"It's because I don't care, sis. I think I stopped caring a while ago, but, you know, old habits die hard."

"There must be something there, surely? I mean, from what Brie told Ryker when she phoned last night, it sounded as if you went to town on the guy."

I shot her an impish grin. "Didn't know I still had it in me."

She shook her head, but I caught the lift to her lips. "I just want you to be happy. Like I am."

"I know. Look, sis, every word you and Ryker said last night is true. I wish I could just dust myself off and forget what happened to you, but... I can't. Not yet. I do, however, realize that I need to find a way to balance things far better than I have done of late." I curled my fingers around hers. "Let me do this my way. It'll blow itself out eventually, and I'll have no choice other than to let it go. But as long as there's a whisper of a lead, I have to follow it. You understand, don't you?"

Please say yes.

"Anyone would think he kidnapped you and forced you to pee in a bucket," she grumbled, but her expression let me know she was only teasing.

I rose from my chair and hugged her. "You're the most precious thing in my life. Well, you and Ethan, and Mom and Dad, of course. I love all of you to bits."

"What about Ryker?" she asked, her voice muffled against my chest.

"Ryker who?" I replied.

She drew back. "Elliot," she said, a warning tone to her voice.

I laughed. "Where is the fucker, anyway?"

"He went into the office early."

I nodded. "Probably can't wait to shoot an email off to the board telling them I'm off their backs."

"He can do that from his phone," she replied, a broad grin inching across her face.

I stuck out my tongue like I had when we were kids. "Right, I gotta go home and make sure my cheating ex-girlfriend leaves my house and takes all of her shit with her."

"You're seriously kicking her out before she has anywhere else to go?" Athena asked.

"Oh yeah," I said. "And I'll enjoy it, too."

———

I parked Ryker's precious Bugatti outside my house. Served the bastard right for throwing me out of my own business. He was lucky I didn't arrange for a minor scratch to the paintwork on the way over here. Of course, there was still time. I smiled to myself. He'd be furious when he found the note I'd left him in his home office. He never allowed anyone to drive this car. It might be four years old now, but Ryker adored it and treated it like a second baby.

Childish, maybe, but I was in that kind of mood.

I entered the house, and the first person I thought of was Sage. Not Brie. I pictured her ass in those tight pants as she'd gone to talk to her partner and left me alone in the kitchen last night. The NYPD uniform didn't do it for me, but on Sage, I might make an exception.

I rounded the corner and almost knocked Brie to the floor. She stumbled backward, and as she straightened, I caught sight of her tear-stained face. I braced myself for a stab of sorrow, but I felt nothing. Zero. Zip.

Actually, that wasn't entirely true. She irritated me.

"What are you still doing here?" I snapped.

"Elliot."

She reached out a hand. I stepped back. Her face crumpled, and more tears fell.

"Please, can we talk?" she sob-hiccupped.

Bone-weary, I shook my head.

"Elliot, please. I still love you."

I held up my palm, cutting her off. "But I don't love you. And I haven't for a long time. I asked you to leave, now leave. You aren't the only one who can call the police, and as of now, you're trespassing. If you don't get your cheating ass off my property, I will call the cops and have you removed."

She gasped. "When did you become so cruel?"

"The second you spread your legs for another man."

I walked off. She followed me, grabbing my arm. I glanced down to where her red-tipped nails clutched my forearm.

"Let go, Brie," I demanded, my tone flat and cold.

"You're looking at me like you hate me."

"I don't hate you. Hate's an emotion steeped in passion. I feel nothing for you other than contempt." I loomed closer, my face mere inches from hers. "Now grab your shit and get the fuck out of my house. I never want to see you again."

She choked out another sob and ran upstairs. Thirty

minutes later, she lugged two suitcases down the stairs. I didn't make a move to help her, just stood with my arms folded, my shoulder propped against the doorjamb, watching her wheel them to the front door.

"I'll send someone for the rest of my things," she said, sniffing.

"Make it in the next twenty-four hours or I'll have them packed up and shipped off to the nearest women's shelter."

Without uttering another word, she stepped outside and closed the door behind her.

And me... I breathed a fucking big sigh of relief.

And that simple reaction told me everything I needed to know.

Chapter Five

SAGE

"ARE YOU SURE YOU'RE GOING TO BE OKAY?"

I bent to kiss Mom's cheek and tweaked my sister, Lily's nose, resulting in a giggle. Anyone looking in would think it strange of me to do such a thing to a grown woman. Despite her birthdate showing her to be almost twenty-three, her brain was stuck as an eight-year-old. The year following my graduation from high school, on her way home from a friend's house, someone had attacked her for no reason, literally sixty seconds from our apartment. The assailant punched the back of her head, sending Lily crashing to the sidewalk. She smashed the front of her skull, leaving her with permanent brain damage.

My original plans after I left school had been to go to college to study architecture—my one true love—but because of what happened to Lily, I'd joined the police academy instead, determined to find the man who'd ruined my sister's future. All these years later, the culprit was still at large, and I'd eventually had to accept that I'd never find him now. Even so, quitting the police and following my dreams was out of the question. The medical insurance provided as part of my job was too good to lose, especially as Lily benefitted from continuing therapy.

"Yes, Sage," Mom said, giving me one of her raised eyebrows that doubled up as a "stop fussing" message. "You work hard. You deserve a little downtime. Cassandra is your best friend. It'll disappoint her if you don't attend her birthday gathering, especially as she's traveled from upstate just so you could go."

I couldn't argue with that. Cassandra had bugged me for days to make sure my shifts lined up so I could attend tonight's bash and get thoroughly sloshed in the process. I had two days off, more than enough to recover from a hangover. Her words, not mine. I planned to take it easy.

"Besides, Lily and I are planning a Disney marathon, aren't we, darling?" Mom cuddled Lily tight to her side, and my sister nuzzled in.

"Yes," she beamed enthusiastically. "It's *Beauty and the Beast* first, isn't it, Mommy?"

"Whatever my angel wants."

My chest tightened. God, I loved these two. Mom was my rock, Lily my whole life. My mind turned to Dad. He'd died when Lily was six, and I was seventeen. I'd lived half my life without him, and I still missed him terribly. But Lily missed him most of all. She'd been such a daddy's girl. One of the side effects of her head injury was struggling with the passage of time so, to her, it often felt as if Dad had only passed recently, and during those episodes, she'd sob for hours, begging him to come back. It broke my heart. Every single time.

"Okay, Lily Billy. You be good for Mom."

She giggled again. "I will."

I picked up my purse from the chair by the window, made sure I had my wallet and keys as well as Cassandra's gift and, shrugging into my coat, I stepped out into the freezing cold. More snow had fallen in the short time I'd been home, and it crunched underfoot as I trudged to the subway.

Cassandra had arranged for us to meet up at a bar in Greenwich Village, an hour away from my home in East Brooklyn. Apparently, it was one of those trendy places— the kind I hated and Cassandra loved. Normally, I'd have declined on that fact alone, but like Mom said, Cass had arranged to have her birthday gathering here principally so I could attend, and I didn't see her nearly enough as it was, on account of the job she secured upstate which took her away from the city. This would be the first time I'd seen her in the flesh in over a year.

A more sensible person would have taken their shit to work and gotten dressed for the evening there, meaning a much shorter commute time of twenty minutes. But that would have meant going all day and all night without visiting home, and I didn't like to do that if I could help it. Not that Mom couldn't cope—of course she could—but I'd always been a worrier when it came to my family, and that would never change.

Riding the subway gave me the first chance I'd had all day to think, and Elliot Bancroft was the place my mind chose to visit. I wondered whether the cold light of day had seen him and his girlfriend patch things up, or if he'd carried out his threat to throw her out onto the street with nowhere to go. He hadn't seemed very affected by her infidelity. Sure, she'd wounded his pride. What guy wouldn't be pissed if they came home and found what Elliot had and maybe lash out with their fists? But that didn't go anywhere near explaining his over-the-top reaction in beating the shit out of the man she'd cheated with. No, something else was behind his rage. The Elliot I'd known at school with the quick smile and sunny personality was the complete opposite to the embittered man I'd arrested last night.

My mind spun back to the month before we graduated. Students had crammed the hallway, moving from one class to another. I'd sidled my way through the throngs, cradling a stack of books to my chest, and someone had bumped into me. I'd fallen flat on my ass, and my books had skidded across the floor where several students trampled them underfoot. Only one person had stopped to help me up: Elliot Bancroft. I could still recall the swarm of butterflies taking flight in my stomach as he'd wrapped his warm, strong fingers around mine and eased me to my feet. Once he'd assured himself I wasn't seriously hurt, he'd picked up all my books and insisted he carry them to class. He wasn't even in my class. At the door, he'd smiled at me, told me to have a good day, and left. That was the last time I'd spoken to him—until last night.

At least I'd held my own. I'd long since left that gawky, shy girl behind. Years spent dealing with murderers, rapists, burglars, and drug addicts, to name but a few, had knocked every bit of introversion out of me. These days, I was far more confident, both in and out of work. In a way, choosing this career path had been the making of me. If I'd gone to college and followed my architectural dreams, I'd lay odds on still being that awkward, nervous girl who blended into the background.

I bowed my head against the driving wind and flurries of snowflakes and jogged the five minutes between the subway station and the bar. I arrived slightly out of breath and burst through the doors like a whirlwind. I brushed the snow off my coat and hung it on an anthracite stand, then scanned the room. Cassandra had commandeered a huge corner booth, and she waved madly as she spotted me. I weaved between packed tables and knocked a woman's jacket off the back of a chair. I bent down, picked it up, and put it back without her noticing.

"You made it!" Cassandra squealed, wrapping me in a tight hug that almost cut off my air supply. "God, I've missed you. FaceTime just isn't the same."

"I've missed you, too," I said. "Although you're lucky I love you." I gestured around at the upper-class clientele enjoying over-priced steaks and cocky Wall Street types lining the bar. "Here, really?"

"It's the place to be to snag a rich husband," she explained, completely unfazed by the inappropriateness of her comment. "Seriously, Sage, New York Magazine featured *the owner* last month. He's a real up-and-comer in the hospitality industry." She eyeballed the joint. "Single, too, apparently."

I chuckled at her frankness and said hi to the rest of the girls. Most of them were from Cassandra's old workplace before she'd moved upstate, but I'd met them all on several occasions in the past. I'd known Cassandra for six years. We met when I got a call out to investigate a burglary at her apartment. Somehow, we'd clicked, and had remained close friends from that day to this.

Cassandra poured me a margarita from a pitcher in the center of the table and tugged me to sit next to her.

"Here," I said, producing her badly wrapped gift. "Happy Birthday, Cassie."

She dug me in the ribs. Her grandmother insisted on calling her Cassie, and she hated it.

"Bitch." She tore off the paper. "This'd better be good after that insult." She opened the box and gasped at the solid silver bracelet nestled in folds of blue satin. "Oh, Sage. You shouldn't have. It's too much."

"Nonsense." It'd taken me months to save up. I'd put a little aside out of every paycheck, but Cass was worth it. I removed the bracelet and slipped it around her wrist. "There. It looks great on you."

She hugged me and rested her head on my shoulder. "Love you."

The gossip began in earnest, and I listened with half an ear, letting most of it wash over me. One of the many things that worked with Cassandra and me was how we were diametrically opposite. But when I was surrounded by duplicates of her, all of whom only seemed interested in talking about men and makeup, well, it became a little tedious after a while. Snagging a guy was so far down my list of priorities, my pen had run out of ink by the time I got there.

"Oh. My. God!"

Cassandra's shriek jerked my attention away from a couple outside who were in the middle of a heated argument.

"Look at him! My ovaries are weeping over here. He's gorgeous."

In unison, all of us, including me, turned our heads to follow Cassandra's excited gaze. When my eyes landed on the guy who'd caught her attention, I groaned.

You have got to be kidding me.

What the hell was Elliot doing here? Then again, he fit in far better in a place like this than I did. He strode confidently over to the bar and shared a word with the bartender, then took a seat and checked his watch, as if he was waiting for someone. I mused about whether he was waiting for his girlfriend, and they had made it up after all, or if he was expecting someone else. A different woman, maybe. A sliver of disappointment settled in my chest, one that had no right to be there.

He scanned the bar, and his gaze settled on me. His eyebrows shot up, then he smiled and got to his feet. I turned away quickly.

Don't come over here. Don't come over here. Don't come...

"Officer Abbott. What a pleasant surprise."

Cassandra inhaled sharply, and the rest of the girls around the table all stared at me, then him, then back at me. I groaned again. *Just great.*

"Mr. Bancroft. I hope you're staying out of trouble this evening."

He chuckled. "Doing my level best, Officer."

Cassandra gave me a sharp dig in the side, a not-so-subtle hint to introduce her. When I failed to, she thrust out her hand. "I'm Cassandra Bailey, Sage's—I mean Officer Abbot's—best friend. It's very nice to meet you."

I rolled my eyes at her blatant come-on. Elliot, though, appeared unperturbed. He shook her hand and smiled at the rest of the gawping women. "Nice to meet you. Would you mind awfully if I steal Officer Abbott for a few moments? I need a quick word."

A wide grin spread across Cassandra's face. "Of course not."

She followed that up with a second jab in the ribs. I swear she was trying to crack one. I glared at her. She responded with an overexaggerated wink.

Reluctantly, I got to my feet and trailed after Elliot, who retook his seat at the bar. He tugged the chair next to him a little closer meaning, as I climbed up, our knees brushed together.

"Sorry," I said, angling my legs to the side.

"Don't apologize on my account," he said, those gorgeous eyes of his searching my face. For what, I didn't have a clue, but I found myself unable to tear my gaze away all the same.

"What can I do for you?" I asked formally as a way to distract myself from the horde of butterflies swarming my stomach. *Get a grip, Sage.* It didn't matter how attractive Elliot Bancroft was, he and I swam in different oceans. Not to mention the man came with more baggage than a luggage store, and I had more than enough going on in my life than to hook up with a guy like him.

Look at you, Miss Arrogant. Elliot hadn't shown any interest in me romantically. He'd been too busy trying to deal with the broken pieces of his shattered relationship.

"How are you?" he asked.

Thrown off-kilter at his unexpected question, I frowned. "I'm okay."

"So, a cop, huh? What diverted you from becoming an architect?"

Right, hold the phone. How the hell did he know I'd wanted to be an architect? And what exactly was going on here?

"Forgive me, Mr. Bancroft, but I'm confused. You invited me over here to reminisce?"

He groaned. "Can we stop with the Mr. Bancroft, Officer Abbott shit? It's not like we're strangers."

I rubbed my lips together. "Aren't we? It's not like we

were bosom buddies in high school either. You never even knew I existed."

"Says who?" he replied. "I know more than you think."

Yeah, like my dreams of becoming an architect.

"Want to know a secret, Sage?"

I sighed heavily. "I'm not really into game playing, so if you have something to say, I suggest you get on with it."

Elliot chuckled. "Wow. You are so different from the scared little mouse in high school. I love it. And as for the game playing, some of them can be fun."

He waggled his eyebrows.

I rolled my eyes.

"Do you always talk in riddles with an added dash of innuendo?"

"Sometimes."

"Well do us both a favor and stop. You're not original. I've heard it all in my time on the force."

He hissed. "Ouch. Your tongue burns."

"I don't have time to play games, Mr. Bancroft." I cast a guilty glance at Cass who nodded in approval and flicked her wrist at me in a 'keep going' gesture. I disagreed. "I'm out with my friends tonight, so I'll be seeing you."

I made a move to stand.

His hands landed on my thighs, holding me in place. "Wait, please."

Heat from his palms seeped through my pants, and a shiver of delight echoed down my spine. I glowered at him, my message clear. *Remove your hands or lose them.* A reflex rather than a desire. I liked his hands on me. Far, far too much.

He let me go and straightened. "Sorry, that was an over-reach. I don't mean to come across as a gigantic asshole."

I flashed another glance at Cass. This time, she made a rude sexual gesture. I quickly averted my gaze. Elliot sniggered.

"Your friend is quite the character."

Heat bloomed in my cheeks. I'd kill her.

"She has her moments," I murmured. "I really do have to go."

"I got a fine," he said.

I paused, confused, and then caught on to his meaning. "You must have had a sympathetic judge."

"It's the charmer in me," he said, and the way his lips lifted at the corners gave me a hint of the young man I remembered—and the young me reacted. My stomach twisted, and I automatically pressed my legs together to ease the growing ache there.

"Yes, well, maybe next time, keep your fists to yourself." I jumped off the stool. "Good luck, Elliot."

"Wait." He reached for me, then thought better of it. "Would you like to go out for a drink or a bite to eat some-time? On a night when you're not otherwise engaged. It'd be great to catch up. I'm not in touch with many people from high school."

I opened my mouth to decline, but my brain had other ideas.

"Sure, why not?"

His smile extended right up to his eyes, and it pleased me more than it should. More than it was safe to. Elliot Bancroft had trouble written all over him, and I'd willingly stepped into his realm.

"What food do you like? I'll book somewhere."

Too late to back out now, Sage.

"Um, I know a decent bistro close to me, over in Brooklyn. If that isn't too far." My territory. A way for me to assert control over a rapidly spiraling situation. One I hadn't expected when I rode the subway over to Manhattan this evening.

"Not too far at all."

He slipped his hand into the inside pocket of his suit jacket and passed me a business card. I glanced down at the thick, expensive card and scanned his contact details.

"Call me or drop me a text. Whichever suits you."

"Okay." I caught Cass's eye as I walked away. She gave me two thumbs-up and a goofy grin. As I slid alongside her, she almost broke my rib with her elbow.

"Score!" she announced, loud enough for the entire bar, including Elliot, to hear.

I groaned for the third time in less than fifteen minutes. *Just marvelous.*

Chapter Six

ELLIOT

AFTER THE LONGEST WEEK OF MY SORRY-ASS LIFE, where the most exciting thing to happen was when Brie sent a friend to pick up the last of her things, I drove over the Brooklyn Bridge toward Sage's place in East Brooklyn for our date.

I didn't care how far I had to travel. If she told me to meet her in Outer Mongolia, I'd have jumped on a plane in a heartbeat. I'd silently thanked Oliver a million times for choosing that bar to meet up. Ever the nice guy, he'd wanted to check on me given my enforced sabbatical from the ROGUES board. Not that I'd paid him much attention from the moment he'd sat his butt in the chair Sage had vacated. I'd been too busy sneaking glances at her celebrating with her friends. Strangely, she'd appeared to be the odd one out, hardly engaging in conversation. She'd just let it all swarm around her, occasionally nodding and taking the occasional sip of a margarita she struggled to reach the bottom of.

Cars parked on either side of the street made negotiating

the limited space difficult, and my car stuck out like a horny teenage boy's dick at an all-girl's school recital. Gangs hung around, their eyes following me as I drove by, scanning for Sage's apartment block. Maybe I should've chosen a vehicle that didn't scream wealth, but... well... I didn't own one. Mom had kept the car she'd bought me as a graduation present for sentimental value, but that would've meant tracking over to their house to pick it up, and honestly, it hadn't occurred to me until now.

I found her place without too much trouble and parked. I admit I hesitated at leaving my beloved Aston Martin alone on the street, but there weren't a lot of other choices at my disposal. I should've hung on to Ryker's Bugatti a little while longer. I chuckled, thinking back to his fury when he discovered I'd taken it. Served the bastard right. I was still pissed at him for throwing me out on my ass, even if in my more somber moments, I secretly admitted to myself that I'd have done exactly the same in his shoes.

I reached the elevator, but before I pressed the button, Sage's voice came from behind me.

"Elliot."

I turned around in time to see her stroll toward me. Warmth engulfed my chest as I ran my gaze over her. She'd curled her golden hair over her shoulders, and her eyes, a smoky gray, were framed with dark lashes that looked too long to be real. She'd added a dash of color to her lips but left her face bare of the thick layer of makeup most women I came across seemed to favor. It only made her more attractive, at least to me.

And that body—encased in skintight jeans, a fitted emerald-green sweater, and black low-heeled ankle boots—

hot damn. Probably just as well the NYPD uniform didn't accentuate her curves. It'd only invite a shitload of trouble.

"Hey," I said, trying to sound casual and failing miserably. The huskiness to my voice and the way my eyes seemed to have a mind of their own, roving over her as if she were the first female I'd ever seen, all conspired to give me away.

"You found me okay, then?"

"Ah, yeah. No trouble. The car's right outside."

I walked slightly ahead of her, down the narrow path and back to where I'd left the car—if someone hadn't robbed it. Thankfully, there it was, right where I'd left it, and without any scratches to the paintwork.

"You brought that. Here?" Sage asked. "Wow. You're lucky I'm not having to call in a stolen vehicle."

I laughed and opened the door for her. "Plenty more where this came from."

Bancroft, you jerk. Look where she lives.

I shot her an apologetic grin that I hoped meant she'd cut me some slack. "And I just realized how much of a dick that comment made me sound like."

She smiled softly, and the dick I'd just mentioned jumped inside my jeans. My fingers itched to trace her full lower lip, to see if it felt as soft as I imagined. There'd always been something special about her. Different from the typical high school teenage girl. All these years later and that hadn't changed. Sage Abbott effortlessly stood out in a crowd, and yet she didn't have a fucking clue.

"Even back in high school, I never had doubts you'd make it, Elliot. You weren't like all the others. There was a steeliness about you, a determination to succeed. The fact you have only reaffirms the beliefs I had all those years ago."

She climbed into the car and tugged the door closed. I strode around to the driver's side.

"We had a fair chunk of luck along the way," I said, firing up the engine.

"I'd love to hear about it."

Before I pulled away, I shifted in my seat to get a better look at her. "I'd rather hear about you."

She picked at a loose thread on the hem of her sweater. "It's all rather boring."

"I'll be the judge of that," I said. "Now, where's this bistro?"

She gestured for me to drive. "I'll direct you."

It took us ten minutes to arrive at the restaurant. The server seated us over by the window in a booth made for six. I waited for Sage to choose a side, then slid along the other bench. We ordered drinks. I stuck to soda, considering I had a cop sitting across from me. She chose a bottle of beer. As the server retreated, I latched my eyes on to hers.

"I never got to tell you my secret," I said, my lips curving into a faint smile.

"Huh?" She frowned. "You've lost me."

"The other night at the bar. I asked you if you wanted to know a secret, and you accused me of playing games."

She arched a perfectly plucked eyebrow. "And you're still playing them a week later, I see."

I chuckled, relishing how she called me out and seemed mildly irritated by me. All that did was make me want to win her over.

"I had a huge crush on you in high school."

Her lips parted, and she blinked several times. "You did not."

"I did. Why would I lie?"

45

"I'm not sure." She eyed me with suspicion. "Something tells me you're used to using the truth sparingly in order to get your own way."

I pressed a hand to my chest. "Sage Abbott. You wound me."

She snorted. "You're still cute, but I'm far too jaded to fall for your charms."

"You think I'm cute?" I waggled my eyebrows. "Excellent."

Tracing a scratch on the table with her fingernail, she averted her gaze. "I'm sorry about your girlfriend."

I chuckled. "Expertly crafted diversion. Spoken like a true cop."

Her chin came up, and her eyes locked on mine. Damn, I could spend days drowning in their charcoal-gray depths. Silent seconds scraped by as we looked at each other, and it felt as though she was sizing me up, trying to figure me out. *Good luck with that.* If she managed it, I'd ask her to explain it to me. These days I barely recognized myself from the jovial guy I'd once been.

"That must've been tough. To come home and find her... well..."

"Fucking someone else?" I smiled to soften my words. "The honest truth is that I don't care. I haven't cared in a really long time, but like most people, I guess it was easier to stay in a poor relationship than go through the hassle of breaking things off."

"Were you together a while?"

I paused while the server set down our drinks and picked up a menu to show her we hadn't decided on food yet. She got the message, retreating to check on another table. "About four and a half years."

"That's a long time."

I shrugged. "I guess."

"There must be some part of you that's sad it's over?"

"If you must know, the overwhelming feeling is one of relief."

She angled her head to the side, her eyes roving over my face. "What happened to you, Elliot? And I'm not talking about your girlfriend. There's something... oh, I don't know. It's as if you're having to work really hard to contain yourself. Like at any moment, you might explode and flatten everything in a five-mile radius. Which is odd, considering not only your clear success, but back in high school you were one of the most relaxed guys around."

Her astuteness in nailing my inner struggle got to me, her comments a little too close to the growing concerns I had about my mental state. And so I deflected. No, not deflected. I snapped at her.

"Everyone changes. That's life."

A mask slid over her face, and she looked at me for a beat, then removed a plastic menu from the slot and opened it. We descended into silence. A useful weapon, one she no doubt used to great effect in her everyday life. I closed my eyes slowly and released a long sigh.

"I'm sorry. You're right. I am different."

She closed the menu and leaned back against the bench. "I'm not here to pry, Elliot. It was an observation, that's all. If you don't want to talk about it, that's fine by me. It's none of my business."

Talking. Something I'd done less and less of as the years had crawled by. Each dead end resulted in me retreating further into the abyss. I was clinging on by my fingernails, the excessive use of my fists on Brie's lover a testament to that.

"Four years ago, an unknown assailant snatched my sister off the street and held her captive for over twenty-four hours," I blurted. "Doesn't sound like very long, but when it happens to someone you love, it's a fucking lifetime. We paid a fifty million dollar ransom—against law enforcement advice—and the perp let her go. I've spent the last four years chasing every lead to find the man who took her. So far..." I threw my hands out to the sides. "Nada."

Her eyebrows shot up toward her hairline, a clear sign that whatever she'd expected me to say, it wasn't that. She tugged repeatedly on her bottom lip, and I almost groaned. She oozed sensuality. Gone was the timid girl who'd barely spoken above a whisper, her voice easily carried away by the hustle and bustle of school hallways, and in her place was a confident woman who I'd really like to get close to, in all the important ways.

"That's gotta be rough. How's your sister coping?"

I snorted a bitter laugh. "That's the rub. She's fine. Happily married to my best friend, and they recently had a baby. A little boy. Ethan. No, Athena has moved on with her life just fine. It's me who's fucked up." I scrubbed both palms over my face. "I'm spiraling down a deep well, Sage, and the sides are so smooth, I have nothing to grab a hold of."

My voice sounded hollow, mirroring the hole in my chest. Sage narrowed her eyes, still tugging on her bottom lip. Damn, I wanted to kiss her. To lose myself in her. To feel something for once. Instead, I diverted my attention to the menu.

"Steak looks good." When a reply wasn't forthcoming, I

lifted my head. "Of course, looks can deceive," I added with a faint smile.

"Can I ask you something?"

"Do you have to?" I smiled, then gestured with my hand. "Go for it."

"Is the obsession with finding the perpetrator who abducted your sister for you, or for her?"

"Her," I replied instantly. "I want her to feel safe, to know that the person who did that to her is behind bars where he belongs."

She twisted her lips to the side. "Sounds to me as if she's doing just fine. My advice, for what it's worth, is that you need to examine your motivations. That'll take some self-reflection and honesty, but until you uncover the real drive for continuing this quest, the bottom of that well is only going to get closer. And trust me, you really don't want to land there."

My vision clouded, and a quiver shot down my spine at her sheer audacity. It was on the tip of my tongue to tell her she knew nothing about my motivations, but I reined it in, forced myself to take a moment, and that pause gave me time to reflect, to replay every word she'd spoken. I skimmed my hand along my jaw. Why was I so insistent on continuing to search, given the enormous impact it had started to have on my life? I'd lost my girlfriend, and while our relationship had been on the rocks for a while, a good part of the reason for that was my continuing obsession, dashing off at a moment's notice when the team of people I had searching came up with a clue that turned out to be nothing. I'd been kicked out of my own company for losing a major deal, and that stung like a motherfucker. I'd let down my friends who deserved so much better. But most of all, I'd lost myself.

Yet despite the enormous cost, I knew I'd never let this lie. Not completely. Even if I reached ninety, it'd still be there at the back of my mind, gnawing at me. The question was, why?

"Sorry if that came out a bit blunt." Her lips curved ever so slightly. "It's the cop in me."

I blinked, then drew in a ragged breath. "I think you raise a pertinent question. Except I don't have an answer."

The server headed toward us again, but a brief shake of my head sent her into retreat.

"You're her brother. It's natural to want to protect her."

I hitched up my shoulder. "Yeah."

"I'm sure your father feels the same way."

"He's far calmer than me," I said, flashing a quick grin. Dad was with Athena on this. He'd quietly berated me several times for obsessing over what had happened. "So relaxed he's horizontal most days."

As the words left my lips, a horrific thought snapped inside my head, and my lungs flattened. Dad was a quiet, measured guy, but my birth father wasn't. Oh Christ. Maybe I was like that bastard after all. My greatest fear, that nature would overtake nurture and turn me into a replica of that monster, coming true.

"You've gone awfully pale, Elliot. Are you okay?"

I swallowed and dampened my lips. "Did you know I was adopted?"

She shook her head, containing any surprise she might have felt, and remained silent, waiting for me to continue.

"My birth father used to beat my mother. Badly. When I was eight, he put her in the hospital. That was the catalyst for her to finally pluck up the courage to leave. After the doctors released her, she sat me down, her face black and blue, her arm in a cast, and told me that things were going to get better, and that now, I was the man of the house. That I needed to help her take care of Athena, who was only two at the time."

I gave a half shrug as if sharing that private detail hadn't really bothered me when, in reality, I hated talking about that shit. It was a dark time, a tough time, until Mom met Karl, the man I thought of as my real dad, and our lives changed significantly for the better.

"Then Mom met Karl, and he adopted us."

Her eyes searched my face. "Yet you continued to hold on to the responsibility for your sister. You set yourself up as her protector and now feel culpable over her abduction. That's not the case, Elliot. The only man at fault here is the one who took her. You didn't cause her suffering. He did." She covered my clenched fists with her hand. "Sometimes we have to just let things go."

I stared at our connection, bathing in her warmth. I freed one of my hands and brought it over the top of hers. She remained there for a few moments, then withdrew.

"Did you keep in touch with your birth father?"

I laughed bitterly. "Hell, no. He got a twelve-year stretch for what he did to Mom. About a year following his release, he came sniveling around, right after my company, ROGUES, hit the big time. Said he'd discovered God while he was inside and that his faith had changed him." I snorted. "And then he asked me for money to help him get back on his feet."

"And did you help him?"

"Not a fucking chance. The only thing he got from me was a broken nose."

Sage's lips curved slightly. "I'm sensing a theme."

I ground my teeth together, a standard response reserved for my sperm donor. I'd stopped thinking of him as a father long ago. "Given recent events, you might be forgiven for thinking I often go around leading with my fists. I don't, unless you hurt someone I love and then you'd better watch your back because I don't let that shit lie."

"Like Brie?" she asked gently.

I shook my head. "That's completely different."

"Is it?"

"Yes," I snapped. And then I sighed heavily and let go of the napkin I hadn't realized I'd screwed into a ball. "Look, what went down with that dude had more to do with a dent to my ego than love for Brie. No man likes to think his girl would cheat. In my opinion, cheaters are lowlifes. She could have broken things off with me and then she'd have been free to fuck whoever she wanted, but to cheat? Nah. Not cool. Unforgiveable."

We slipped into silence, which allowed the server to take our food order. Once she left us alone, Sage gave my hand another squeeze. A brief touch, but one that sent pleasure rushing through my veins.

"I do understand, Elliot. That burning need to find the man who took your sister, who caused such pain and anguish to your family."

People always said that, but they didn't. Not really. Only when someone you loved most in the world was badly hurt could others truly understand. But I saw no reason to squish Sage's attempts at empathy.

"Yeah."

"I'm not just saying that. I really do understand."

She grabbed her beer bottle by the neck and tipped it up to her lips. When she set it down, she picked at the corner of the label where condensation helped it to come easily away from the bottle.

"A year after I graduated, CCTV caught a guy thumping my sister in the back. She fell, hit her head, and sustained a catastrophic brain injury. He left her lying there on the cold, wet ground. She's almost twenty-three now, but her mental age is closer to eight, the age she was when it happened."

I leaned in. "Oh, God."

She locked her bleak gaze on to mine and shrugged. "They never caught him. It's something I've had to learn to live with. It hasn't been easy, but after so many years, I had no option other than to let it go. We moved soon afterward to where we live now. I didn't want any of us, but especially Lily, to be reminded of that day."

In that moment, I understood her reason for sharing her heartbreak as well. She'd done it for me, to show me that sometimes, no matter how much we wished for a different outcome, we didn't always get what we wanted. And then another revelation washed over me.

"And that's why you joined the police rather than studying architecture as you'd planned."

She nodded, adding a redundant, "Yup. After it happened, I dropped out. I thought I'd stand a better chance of nailing the guy from inside the police force. Turns out I'm just as impotent. On the upside, the medical coverage meant that Lily got the long-term help she needed."

Sitting opposite Sage as she shared such a horrible experience, an interview with one of my idols, a star hockey player paralyzed in a car accident, came back to me. He said that no matter how bad you have it, there's always someone worse off than you.

And finally, I truly appreciated what he meant.

Chapter Seven

SAGE

YEARS HAD PASSED SINCE I'D TOLD ANYONE WHAT happened to Lily, mainly because retelling the events of that day sent me hurtling back to a time so horrendous, I'd chosen to push it far into the deepest recesses of my mind. The hours pacing the hospital while we waited for them to drain the blood from her brain, and then the days following where neither Mom nor I had gotten any sleep as we'd prayed for her to wake up from the coma. And when she had, her—and our—true horror had begun. As soon as the doctors told us it was likely she would always remain locked in the mind of an eight-year-old and all the challenges that would bring as she grew, I'd immediately dropped out of college and applied to join the police academy.

Yet after a short time in Elliot Bancroft's company, I'd so easily spilled my guts.

What was it about this guy that made me want to put my arms around him and never let go? Perhaps the similarities to our stories connected us in a way that automatically brought us closer, the kind of closeness that usually took years to build. Or maybe having the guy I'd lusted after in my formative teenage years tell me he had a crush on me had sent my lady bits into rapture, resulting in a brain-to-mouth malfunction. Whatever the hell was going on, I instinctively knew that a rush of danger was bearing down on me, and I had no plans to leap out of the way. Instead, I met it head-on.

"Let me help you."

Elliot's mouth creased in thought, and he scratched his cheek. "With what?"

"Finding Athena's kidnapper."

His eyebrows shot upward as my meaning became clear. "Why would you do that?"

The label came away from my beer, and I folded it into a square and set it to one side. "I know what it's like to want revenge so badly, it's all you can think about. Day, night, weekends, holidays. It uses you up, and the accompanying loneliness steals the person you were until you don't recognize yourself any longer. But trust me, Elliot, that path leads to ruin. I will do what I can to help you, but it comes with a condition and a warning."

He set those amber eyes on me, and I knew that if I let him, he'd drown us both. Except right now, I'd happily loop my arms around his neck and let him pull me beneath the water. He had that kind of power over me, suppressed for years, but now that he'd exploded back into my life, that power had returned with a vengeance.

Elliot quirked an eyebrow and waited for me to continue. I shoved aside thoughts that getting into bed with Elliot Bancroft—physically or metaphorically—was just about the worst idea I'd ever had. Too late now. I must have a death wish.

"First, the warning. There are absolutely no guarantees. Like any crime, the more time that passes, the less chance there is of finding the perpetrator, and after four years, our chances are slim to almost none. You need to be prepared for that."

"And the condition?"

"We give it three months. I'll do whatever I can to help you sort through the clues and follow up on any leads, but at the end of that time, if we're no further forward, you agree to drop it and move on with your life."

I'd added the time-limited condition for two reasons: one, it'd allow me to get to know Elliot as the man he now was rather than the high school crush I'd known fifteen years ago. Call me crazy, but given the fact my heart hadn't slowed down from the moment I'd seen him standing by the elevator looking good enough to eat, and the way I kept pressing my thighs together to relieve a growing heaviness at my core, the feelings I'd had for Elliot hadn't gone away. They'd remained suppressed, like a virus, and now he'd shown up again the damn things were running rampant. The problem was, whatever he said about his girlfriend and not being sad about the breakup, I'd seen enough rebound relationships crash and burn not to want to add myself to the statistical pool.

The second reason for the condition was that I wanted him to recognize he might fail—an alien concept to a man as successful as he was—but that didn't mean he was a failure. I guess I didn't want him to waste his life on a pointless quest.

He pondered for close to a minute. Unsurprising, considering he'd always been reflective, the sort of man who wouldn't make rash promises he either didn't think he could keep or had no intention of keeping in the first place. If he agreed to my condition, then he was all in. If he didn't, that was on him. Either way, I refused to budge.

He held out his hand. "Deal."

I shook it, savoring the feel of his skin against mine. Only when he chuckled did I realize I hadn't let go.

"Sorry."

His amber eyes darkened, almost like the embers of a fire once the initial flames had diminished. "Don't be."

I withdrew anyway, considering if I should sit on the damn things. That might stop them from itching to stroke his warm cheek, or feel the cords of muscle beneath his shirt, or slip lower to...

"Thank you."

His warm baritone jerked me from my dirty thoughts, but that didn't stop a flush of heat pinking my cheeks. Thankfully, we were sitting in a dark corner of the restaurant, the ambient lighting covering my blushes—literally.

"What for?"

He sighed heavily. "It's been a lonely road."

I arched an eyebrow. "Maybe that's because it's filled with potholes."

His faint smile, tinged with sadness, made me wish I hadn't replied so flippantly.

"You're right." He straightened, and a determined look appeared on his face. "One last shot, yeah?"

I picked up my beer bottle and tapped it against his glass. "Here's to success."

Our food arrived, but we both picked at it. "Not hungry?" I asked after he'd pushed his fries around his plate without eating a single one.

"Not particularly."

"Me neither." I dropped my fork. "Want to get out of here?"

"And go where?"

I winked. "Let's go have some fun."

———

"Bowling?" Elliot grinned when he realized our destination. "I haven't been bowling in years."

"Yeah? Then prepare for humiliation."

I slid from the car and waited for him to join me. As we strode across the lot toward King Pins, Elliot knitted his fingers with mine. I side-eyed him.

"Don't get any ideas. The nicer you are to me, the more ruthless I become."

He laughed. "You're talking to a billionaire, darlin'," he drawled, faking a Southern accent. "Ruthless is my middle name."

"Yeah? Then let's see what you've got."

We sauntered inside and only had to wait five minutes for a lane to come free. I smiled when we were told to head to lane six—my lucky number. Elliot Bancroft was about to get his ass handed to him, and I'd enjoy every moment.

I annihilated him in the first game, bowling six strikes and three spares. As I set us up for the second, Elliot cracked his knuckles.

"I went easy on you first time around. This time, you're going down, Abbott."

"Not something I like to do in public." I clapped a hand over my mouth, mortified. "Shit. That came out all wrong."

Elliot doubled over laughing. I mean, he really let go, like the kind of laughter that exploded, and you simply couldn't help joining in. By the time we both recovered, my abs felt as if I'd done a thousand sit-ups.

"Fuck." Elliot wiped his eyes. "I haven't laughed like that in years."

"Now's probably a good time to tell you that I do occasionally suffer from brain-to-mouth malfunction."

"Keep 'em coming," Elliot said. "It's been a long time since I felt this good."

Although he spoke with a quirk of the lips, the truthfulness of what he'd shared hit me squarely in the gut, and my face grew serious.

"Whatever happens, it'll be fine, Elliot. *You* will be fine."

He glanced down, his teeth grazing over his bottom lip. And then he caught both my hands in his. "There are several reasons I don't regret busting that jerkoff's nose, but the number one reason is that it brought you back into my life."

My mind screamed *danger*. My heart yelled *take a fucking risk*. And I didn't know which one to listen to. So I did what came naturally in awkward situations. I made a joke.

"Let's revisit that thought after you've been stuck with me for a little while."

His fingers squeezed mine, and his eyes almost bored through me.

"I don't think I'll regret it."

"Yeah, well..." At risk of standing on tiptoes and planting one on him, I let him go and took a step back. "Ready for that second game?"

He gave me a crooked smile, steeped in politeness rather than happiness. "Sure thing."

We played a second, and then a third. On each occasion, I trounced him and, finally, Elliot held up his hands.

"That's it. I'm done. Losing is bad for my ego."

"Never took you for a quitter, Bancroft."

"Hey, even I know when I've been trounced. No point in beating a dead horse." He angled his head to one side. "Although you should know that after a defeat, I usually come out fighting."

"And you should know, I never run away from a battle. I speed toward it."

"I'm banking on it."

On the drive back to my apartment building, Elliot drifted into silence, and I left him with his thoughts. I couldn't help the odd surreptitious glance at him, though, locked as we were in his cozy car, in such close quarters, with the scent of his undoubtedly expensive cologne tickling my nostrils. Men often improved with age, and Elliot hadn't bucked the trend. There'd always been a gaggle of girls following him and Ryker Stone around school. I bet if they saw him now, they'd burst into spontaneous orgasm.

He found a space right outside my building, but as he went to unclip his seat belt, I stopped him. "Probably best not to risk leaving your car here for a second time."

He smiled and nodded. "I'll wait until you're inside, though."

I clasped a hand to my chest. "Ah, my hero."

He ran his tongue over his bottom lip and I almost leaned forward and sucked on it. I averted my gaze, fast, and reached for the door handle.

"Sage."

I shifted to face him. "Yeah?"

He curved a hand around my neck and pulled me to him. His lips touched mine, more a friendly peck than a passionate embrace, but regardless, a tingling shot through me, right down to the tips of my toes.

"Thank you for agreeing to help."

Ah. Gratitude. That's all it was. Not a desire to start something up. Just as well. I didn't need the indisputable heartache that was bound to follow.

"You're welcome. I'll check my shifts and call you."

I walked up the path to my building and, as difficult as it was, I went inside without looking back.

Chapter Eight

ELLIOT

Four days later, the carpet in my living room damn near worn out from my pacing, the knock I'd waited for came. I strode to the front door and opened it.

"Hi." Sage held up a hand in greeting and shifted from foot to foot, almost as if she felt uncomfortable.

"Hi yourself," I said, adding a smile meant to put her at ease. Despite the banter we'd shared the other night, some of it definitely on the sexual side, I understood why being here, at my home, might put her on edge. I stood back and gestured for her to come in, then took her coat and hung it in the hallway closet.

She glanced around the entranceway. "I meant to say when I was last here, you really have a lovely home."

"Yeah, but you were too busy handcuffing me to compliment my humble abode." I arched a brow and a chuckle left her lips.

"That's what happens when you break the law."

"Hmm." I rubbed the stubble on my chin and grazed my

eyes over her. "If that's the outcome, maybe I'll have to break it again."

She narrowed her eyes in a scolding manner. All her attempt at a rebuke did was send blood rushing to my groin.

"Perhaps you should let the last crime age a bit before you add another misdemeanor, or worse, to the list."

God, she really is magnificent.

"Noted, ma'am." I jerked my head toward the kitchen. "I've got a pot of coffee on."

Her soft-soled shoes squeaked on the floor as she followed me to the rear of the house. She wandered over to the large picture window that overlooked a small courtyard.

"Oh, you have an evergreen magnolia," she said, indicating the tree right outside the window. "They're gorgeous, especially in full bloom."

I opened the fridge and removed a jug of cream. "Is that what it is? The garden was Brie's domain. I prefer the roof terrace."

"There's a roof terrace?"

I held up the jug of cream, and she shook her head. "Yeah. I'd show you the view, but it's a little on the cold side."

"I don't mind the cold. Once we've talked and gone through what you have, I'd love for you to show it to me."

I handed her a steaming cup, and she wrapped both hands around it.

"Sure." I returned the jug to the fridge and grabbed my cup. "Follow me."

I set off upstairs and stopped outside a room on the top floor. I fished in my pocket and produced a key, which also produced a perplexed look from Sage.

"You lock the rooms in your house?"

"Only the ones I don't want my girlfriend to have access to." I shrugged. "Guess I don't need to worry any longer."

I opened the door and motioned for her to go in first. She gasped as she glanced around the walls, every spare inch of space taken up with sticky notes, maps, and Google Earth images. Everywhere I'd been. Every lead I'd followed up. Every piece of information, no matter how small, I'd gathered over the last few years.

I watched from the entranceway while she walked around the entire space, stopping occasionally to read something. Finally, she turned to face me.

"It's certainly thorough. Why did you want to keep this a secret from your girlfriend?"

I lifted my right shoulder. "I'm aware this appears a little... obsessive. She already thought I spent too much time chasing shadows and not enough on her. If she saw the lengths I'd gone to, how this search consumed me, well, she'd have felt vindicated in her beliefs."

"Secrecy isn't a good thing in a relationship."

"Neither is adultery."

She smirked and scratched her forehead, then returned to the wall. "It's going to take me a while to go through all of this to see if you've missed anything." Pivoting, she sat on the floor and crossed her legs, then pointed to the space in front of her. "In the meantime, give me the abridged version."

I remained standing. "Why don't we go downstairs? It's more comfortable than sitting on the floor."

She shook her head. "No. This is where you do your thinking." She pointed again. "Sit."

"It's unsurprising you're a cop," I said, parking my butt. "You have that bossy, 'do as I tell you or I'll draw my gun' vibe going on."

"You'd better believe it. Now, spill. From the beginning."

I set my coffee at my feet and took a deep breath. Talking about that time always messed with my head, and even now, four years later, I didn't like to think back, to relive the horror from when I realized someone had taken Athena.

"She was on her way back to work after taking a lunch break when she felt a sting in her neck, and the next thing she recalled was waking up in a cold, damp room chained to a pipe. The perp demanded payment of a fifty million dollar ransom, and in return, he released her unharmed. All Athena could tell us was that his voice rasped, as though he was a heavy smoker, and that he wore a mask. She also said he had a local New York accent, but that it was a little off, as if he'd spent some time out of the area. The weirdest thing, though, was he told Athena that I owed him. He said I'd ruined his life, and that I had to pay." I took a sip of coffee. "When we got her back, I began the process of following the money trail, but eventually, it disappeared, just like he did."

She glanced around the room, then returned her attention to me. "And where did that search take you?"

"All over," I replied. "Not just here, but overseas, too, mainly Europe. The day I returned home to find Brie fucking her personal trainer, I'd been on another wild goose chase, this time to Switzerland."

She frowned. "And that didn't turn up anything?"

"No."

"What led you to go there?"

"A tip-off from one of the private investigators I've had working on this virtually round the clock. Someone he'd spoken to said that they'd heard this guy mention my name one night in a bar. When we tracked him down, it turned out to be someone I'd met with last year. Apparently, he wasn't too happy with the lack of business I sent his way and was bad-mouthing me to one of his associates." I laughed. "Sore loser."

"And your PI couldn't have found that out without dragging you six thousand miles?"

"Their job is to find the leads. My job is to follow them up." I shrugged. "Call me a control freak, but they don't have the skin in the game that I do."

"Control freak," she said, laughing. "Then again, I have little room to talk. I'm exactly the same. Just ask my partner."

For a split second, I thought she was talking about a boyfriend, and a rush of ice shot through my veins. Then I realized she meant her partner at work.

Interesting reaction.

One to examine later... after she'd gone home.

"I need you to make me a list of everyone that you think you might have pissed off in the five years before your sister was kidnapped. Go back longer if you can remember."

I rose to my feet, crossed the room to the window wall, and removed a sheet of paper from the wall. Handing it to her, I said, "Already done. And I've checked out every single one. No dice."

"I'll recheck," she said unapologetically as she flipped over the paper. "Both sides. Wow. You've annoyed a lot of people."

"Spend enough time around me and you'll see why."

I shot her a crooked smile. She shook her head.

"This should be fun. Just know that if I think you're being a jerk, I won't hold back from telling you."

Pleasure tickled the skin at the back of my neck. "I'm banking on it."

We spent another couple of hours in that room while Sage jotted notes on a pad she'd brought with her and fired a hundred questions my way. Finally, she slipped the pad back into her shoulder bag and stiffly got to her feet.

"I think that's all for now. I'll check out a few things at work and let you know what I come up with. But honestly, Elliot, from what I can gather, you've been pretty thorough. If you ever decide being a billionaire isn't rewarding enough, I can put in a word with my sergeant. The NYPD would snap you up in a heartbeat."

I stood, too, my legs aching from sitting around on the floor. "No offense, but I'll take a hard pass. I'm hoping my current unemployed situation is temporary."

Her face softened, and she brushed a hand over my arm. "That's gotta sting."

I rubbed my lips together. "I deserved it. My mind hasn't been on the job for a while, and losing a big client like I did, I'm surprised Ryker didn't toss me out the window of our building. Although if your paths ever cross and you tell him I said that, it'll be you going out the window."

She giggled, and the sound went right to my cock. Damn, she was fucking adorable. And sexy. And hot. And... not a good idea to tangle up with. Sex would only complicate matters.

My dick did not like this plan.

And neither did I.

I doubted I'd stick to it.

"You do know that threatening a member of law enforcement is a criminal offense? Two for two at the courthouse, Mr. Bancroft, and you're looking at jail time."

Her eyes twinkled, and that giggle came again. I went to reach for her, to snap her to me and kiss her until I ran out of air, but she walked right by me and out into the hallway, glancing back over her shoulder.

"So, how about this roof terrace, huh?"

I shrugged off disappointment—she'd probably done me a favor—and jogged downstairs to fetch her coat and grab one for myself. I led her up past the top floor to the winding staircase that led onto the roof. When I thought back to buying this property, its roof terrace had been the number one selling point. And as I took in Sage's wide-eyed expression at her first view of Washington State Park from up here, I doubled down on that belief.

"Cool, right?"

"It's awesome, Elliot. My sister would love this."

"She's welcome anytime." I sidled up next to her, making sure our shoulders touched. "As are you."

She half twisted her body and tipped her head back. Our eyes met, and we just stood there, silently drinking each other in, an invisible cord drawing us closer together until our lips were mere inches apart.

"This could get complicated," she whispered.

"It could."

"It's a bad idea."

I nodded. "Terrible. The worst."

"I don't want to be the rebound girl."

"You won't be."

She opened her mouth to speak again, and I took advantage, cutting off the words before she could say them. I traced my tongue along her lower lip, relishing the faint taste of coffee. When she trembled, I wrapped my arms around her waist and eased her into me, sharing my warmth with her. I deepened the kiss. Feeling around for her zipper, I slid it down. What the next few hours could contain played like a movie inside my mind. I'd lead her back downstairs and into the nearest room with a bed where I'd spend the entire night making her feel good.

I slipped my hands inside her coat and reached underneath her shirt. Damn, she had terrific tits. Firm, round, soft. I brushed my thumbs over her elongated nipples, and she moaned softly.

And then I found my arms empty and Sage standing several feet away.

"I'm sorry, Elliot. This isn't a good idea. Let's keep things professional, okay? Sorry, but I have to go."

She dashed down the stairs and back into the house. By the time the shock had worn off enough to force my legs to move and I followed her, the sound of the front door slamming filtered up the stairs.

Goddammit.

Chapter Nine

SAGE

I TAPPED MY ELBOW ON THE WINDOW OF BETH'S office and held up our drinks. Grinning, she beckoned me inside. Beth was my closest work friend. We'd joined the academy the same year, and while I'd remained an NYPD officer—through choice—she'd flown up the ranks and last year had gotten promoted to lieutenant. It wouldn't surprise me at all if she made captain before too long. I preferred to pound the streets, to connect with the general public. Out there was where the action was, where I believed I could make a real difference. But Bethany had always been hugely ambitious, and I couldn't be happier she was living her dreams.

I set a caramel Frappuccino with extra whipped cream down in front of her, and she blew me a kiss. "You're an angel."

I removed the plastic lid from my black Americano and blew across the top. "You realize all that sugar will kill you one day."

"Yeah, but by then I'll be old and fat and wrinkled, and I

70

won't care. Life's for living, I say." She stuck her finger in the cream and shoved it in her mouth. "Mmm, that's delish."

"Nice," I said.

"You know me, Sage. I have no decorum."

"Thank God for that." I sighed heavily and slumped in my chair.

"Okay, I got the physical clues. What's up?"

I let my head flop back and stared at a damp spot on the ceiling. Seriously, this building was falling apart. "It's been almost a month, Beth, and still nothing. I've worked every spare minute following up on Elliot's leads, and I've come up with zip. I honestly thought that I'd find something, incorrectly assuming that Elliot must have missed a vital piece of evidence. Yet he hasn't. I've reached an impasse. Where do I go from here?"

Beth leaned forward in her chair and rested her inter-laced hands on the desk. "Sage, you and I both know all too well that far more cases go unsolved than those we bring to a satisfactory conclusion, and cold cases in particular are noto-riously hard to crack."

"I know. I just wanted to help him."

She gave me one of her impish looks. "Help him, or screw him."

I smiled wryly. "A little of both, if I'm honest."

"Ah, a high school crush who stands the test of time. As rare as solving a cold case."

A grin edged across my face. "He's matured beautifully."

Beth flicked her wrist. "I honestly don't know what you are waiting for. If a hot, rich guy who I'd lusted after in high school came back into my life, all you'd see is a blur as I took that boy down."

I laughed. God, I loved Beth. She breezed through life

letting very little bother her. Me, I was a thinker. I reflected on shit until it drove me crazy. And ever since Elliot had kissed me on his rooftop terrace, I'd done my level best to avoid him. I'd wanted to throw caution to the wind, but I couldn't take that ultimate step. Elliot was too dangerous a prospect for me to risk getting crushed. At first he'd tried to call, and when I hadn't picked up, he'd texted. When those went unanswered, too, he'd switched into professional mode, bombarding me with emails asking if I'd thought about this or checked that, his obsession relentless.

"Yeah, something's holding me back. Probably the fact that he only just got out of a long-term relationship."

"One he's admitted had been dead in the water for a long time."

"Yeah, but still... He's so hell-bent on finding out who took his sister that I'm worried if he ever finds the culprit that he'll lose it big time. He has the capability. Look at what he did to the man his girlfriend cheated with. He hides it well, but there are these flashes of anger tempered with a geniality and joviality that sucks you in." I blew out a breath. "It's a heady mix."

"If you want my advice, which you clearly do considering you're here, then strap in." She sipped her coffee, then set the cup down. "Forget it, Sage. You have enough on your plate with the demands of your job here and taking care of your sister and your mom. Add this cold case into the mix—one you're not even getting paid to investigate—and if you're not very careful, you'll hit the wall. Believe me, you don't want to go there. You owe this man nothing. You tried your best, but it's time to let it go."

A tap on the door stopped me from replying, and I

glanced over my shoulder as Murphy, one of my coworkers and an all-round jerk, poked his head inside her office.

"Abbott. You've got a visitor."

"Who?"

He glowered at me. "How the fuck do I know? I'm not your messenger boy. I took the call from the front desk, that's all."

He slammed the door, and I rolled my eyes and got to my feet. "Jerk."

Beth snickered. "You got that right."

I picked up my coffee. "Free for a drink later?"

"Sorry, babe. No can do. The captain has asked me to attend some function at City Hall. Maybe tomorrow, or later in the week."

I tamped down disappointment. "Look at you, highflier."

"Getting there."

I left her to it. I finished my coffee, threw the cup into the recycling bin, and jogged downstairs to the reception area. As I approached the half-glass door, I spied Elliot sitting in one of the visitor chairs, his arms dangling between his spread thighs as he examined the cracked tile floor. Damn. No avoiding him now.

I nodded to the officer manning the front desk, and he pointed in Elliot's direction.

"Hey," I called out.

Elliot's head came up, and a glimmer of a smile touched his lips. "You're a tough woman to track down."

"Yeah. I've been busy."

"So your last email said." His eyes roamed over my face. "Except I call bullshit on your ass."

My eyebrows shot up, and I caught the openmouthed

stare of the officer who suddenly looked a lot more interested in this conversation than he had five seconds earlier. "Excuse me?"

Elliot jerked his chin at the same officer. "You want to talk here or go across the street and grab a coffee?"

Despite having just finished one, I nodded. I owed him an explanation and an update. "Wait here while I go fetch my coat."

I sped back upstairs, and five minutes later, we were heading to the coffeehouse across the street from the station. I snagged a table by the window while Elliot went up to the counter to order the drinks. I studied his straight back, broad shoulders, and dark, neatly trimmed hair, and wished things were different. Or maybe I wished that *I* were different. More like Beth or Cass. Able to say "fuck it" and go get some without thinking past that single moment. It wasn't me, though. I'd had two serious relationships over the past fifteen years—and zero one-night stands.

"Here you go."

Elliot set down two cups filled to the brim, without spilling a drop, then took a seat.

"Thanks."

I leaned forward and gingerly picked mine up, sipping to create some space. It'd be just my luck to spill hot coffee all over me and scald myself.

"How've you been?" Elliot asked.

"Okay, I guess. And I have been busy. I wasn't lying."

"Too busy to answer the phone and have a five-minute conversation?" He whacked a packet of Sweet'N Low against his palm and tore it open, emptying the contents into his drink. "Come on, Sage. What's really going on? Was one kiss from me really enough to send you into hiding?"

"It was more than just a kiss."

"Okay, a kiss and a grope. What would we have called that in high school? Second base? Hardly something to get your panties in a twist about."

"I didn't get them in a twist. I changed my mind, that's all. I don't want things to get complicated. I'm sure you want my focus on searching for Athena's kidnapper."

He made a wry face. "And on that subject?"

I massaged my forehead and sighed. "It's a bust. I can't find anything. I'm sorry, Elliot. I honestly thought I'd uncover something you'd missed, but, like I said back at your place when you showed me that room, you've been incredibly thorough."

He rubbed the stubble on his chin, and an inappropriate thought of what that might feel like between my thighs dropped into my mind. I ducked my head to hide the creeping blush across my cheeks. If he asked, I'd blame it on heat from the coffee.

"There has to be something," he said. "What about if we go through it together? Bounce ideas around. Ask the dumb questions that might just send us off in a different direction."

I paused, my thoughts going to Beth's comments. I hadn't missed anything, and neither had Elliot. To continue searching for something that didn't exist was a fool's errand. But as I took in his earnest expression, mingled with the desperate tone I sensed in his voice, I caved.

"Maybe we could take one more look, although I have to be honest and say I'm at a loss what to do next. I have no more leads, and neither do you."

Elliot's gaze drifted down to my chest. "I have one or two ideas on how to pass the time."

"Elliot!" I scolded. "We just had this conversation."

"No. You had that conversation. I haven't agreed to stop trying to persuade you." His tongue dampened his lips. "You have the best tits I've felt in a very long time."

I laughed. I couldn't help it. The man was unapologetic on every level. "Thanks. I think."

"It's not a compliment I hand out lightly. And it'd be a great shame if a freezing cold fumble was the last time I got to sample them."

"You are incorrigible."

"And persistent." He leaned forward. "Come over to my place for dinner. I'll cook my special firecracker chicken. And if the spicy food gets you all hot and bothered, we have several bedrooms at our disposal."

Exasperated, I touched my palms to my cheeks and shook my head. "I'm not sleeping with you, Elliot."

"You will," he said overconfidently. "Just think, Sage. All those years of pent-up frustration unleashed in a single night of rampant passion."

"I bet you never thought of me once after you left school and went off to college. Come on, admit it."

"As a matter of fact, I did. Admittedly, not so much in the last few years, but in those first months after leaving school, I thought about you a lot, wondering how your architecture major was progressing. Little did I know you'd had to give it up." He stopped teasing, his face growing serious. "I wish I'd known."

"It's okay. I like being a cop."

"Like is great. Lots of people live their entire lives liking their jobs just fine. But passion. Now that's something else entirely. You deserve passion."

"Is that another sexual innuendo?"

"Not this time, no."

He locked his eyes on mine, and I got the distinct impression he wanted to say something else but was holding back. When he didn't speak, I checked my watch, then rose to my feet. "I have to go. I still have a few hours of my shift to run yet."

He stood, too. "Let me know when you're free. Tomorrow?"

I nibbled my lip. "I'm not on shift tomorrow night, but I'll have to make sure Mom isn't working. If she is, I'll have to take care of Lily. I'll text you."

"Sounds great."

"Oh, and Elliot."

"Yeah?"

"This is strictly business. I meant what I said. Either we keep this professional, or I'm out."

I fastened my coat and stuffed my hands into my pockets. As I set off toward the exit, Elliot called out to me.

"Sage."

I pivoted to face him. "Yeah?"

"I've missed you."

I wanted to reply with *I've missed you, too.* Instead, I only smiled and said, "Talk to you later."

Chapter Ten

ELLIO

FOUR FUCKING HOURS.

Four torturous hours before the text I'd been waiting for came in. My fingers shook as I opened it. Jeez, this woman had turned me into a pussy, and I didn't even see it coming.

When I read "Your place. Tomorrow. Seven o'clock," I almost punched the air. She'd given me so many brush-offs this last month that, despite turning up out of the blue at her place of work, I'd expected another.

I wasn't the kind of guy who really obsessed over women I found attractive. I thought about them, of course, but they didn't fill my every waking moment. Yet these last few weeks since reconnecting with Sage, she was on my mind twenty-four-seven. Even during the early days of my relationship with Brie, when I'd honestly believed her to be 'The One,' I'd sometimes gone hours or even days without her crossing my mind, especially if a big business deal stole my attention.

Maybe that was it. Because of my temporary ejection from ROGUES, I didn't have enough occupying my mind and, therefore, allowing thoughts of Sage to run riot.

Yeah, that had to be the reason. It was the only logical explanation for my fascination with a woman I barely knew.

With little to take my mind off a date with Sage—okay, not a date—I went for a long run. With any luck, fatigue would help me sleep tonight. Greeting Sage with bags under my eyes a man of my age shouldn't have wasn't the look I was going for.

Sleeping turned out not to be a problem. Morning, on the other hand, turned into a day where time seemed to go backward, and the amount of pacing I undertook meant I'd have to order a new living-room carpet.

Right on time, Sage knocked at my door. I knew it was her because I'd been rubbernecking out my window for the last hour. I opened it and hit her with my sexiest grin.

"Hey, come on in."

I helped her out of her coat. My gaze automatically dropped to her tits, and my chest got all tight. It seemed as if every time I saw her, she sucked the air from my lungs like a vacuum cleaner switched into high speed.

I know what I'd like her to suck. All I needed was for her to accept the inevitable. We could have a lot of fun together if only she'd give in to a clear attraction to me. She'd made no secret of the fact she thought I was on some sort of rebound, and I understood completely why she'd think that. Hell, if the roles were reversed, I'd arrive at the same conclusion. Except in my case, it wasn't true. In fact, since Brie left, she'd barely crossed my mind, and I certainly hadn't missed her. Sage was the only woman I missed when she wasn't around. I was trying not to let that solitary detail scare the shit out of me.

"I thought we'd eat first."

I led her through to the kitchen and motioned for her to

sit at the table while I served up dinner. As she pulled out a chair, she bent forward, affording me a perfect view down her top. I just about managed to stop a husky groan from loudly broadcasting my pleasure at the fantastic view. I did *not* manage to stop my dick getting so hard that it rubbed against my zipper, and the only way to fix it would be to shove my hand down my pants and help it along—which was not happening.

Fuck my life.

I busied myself with serving up the food and, fortunately for me, by the time I set her meal in front of her, my erection had waned to a semi—much easier to hide.

"Wine?" I picked up the bottle of white and poured her a glass without waiting for a response. I'd also put water on the table, so it was her choice of which to drink. She chose the wine, taking a healthy swig.

"God, I needed that."

"Bad day?"

"Just long. Lily had a rough night. I stayed up to sit with her. Mom offered to take shifts with me, but knowing I was coming here, I thought it better she get some sleep in case it happens again."

"You should have cancelled." *I'm glad you didn't cancel.*

"It's fine. I'm used to running on empty."

"Does that happen often? For her to have a disturbed night's sleep?"

"Sometimes." She stabbed her fork tines into a sprig of broccoli and chewed slowly. "She has nightmares occasion-ally, but she never articulates what they're about. When they occur, though, we can't leave her alone. She sobs almost uncontrollably." Her face twisted in pain. "It's heart-wrenching to see."

"I really am sorry that happened to your sister."

She lifted her eyes to mine. "Life is unfair, Elliot. It's a lesson some of us, unfortunately, learn more than others."

"I'd love to meet her. Maybe we could take her on a trip when the weather improves. The Cape perhaps."

She smiled softly. "She loves the beach. I took her to the Jersey Shore last summer, and she played in the sand for hours."

"Then we should make a weekend of it."

Her gaze grew wistful. "The last time we went on vacation was when my dad was still alive. Lily was five, and I was sixteen. He volunteered for as much overtime as his company would give him and saved for a year to take us to Disney World in Florida. I have such fond memories of that trip. Soon afterward, life turned to shit. Dad had a heart attack and died, then Lily's assault happened three years later."

"And you had to give up your dreams."

She shrugged. "Like I said, life is unfair."

A weird sensation lodged in my gut, and a need to make it all better appeared out of nowhere.

"Let me help," I blurted. "You're helping me. It only seems fair I return the favor."

She frowned, and all I wanted was to put my lips on the tiny indents between her eyebrows. "What do you mean?"

"I can pay for you to go to college to study architecture."

Her rebuttal came so fast my head spun. "No. Absolutely not. Besides, it's far too late for me now, and Lily requires ongoing care. If I left the NYPD, then my medical coverage would lapse."

"I can pay for that, too."

"No, Elliot." She made a karate chop motion with her hand as it sliced through the air. "I take care of my family. I don't need you swooping in like a white knight and trying to solve problems that are nothing to do with you."

"I'm more like a dark devil," I said, realizing I'd fucked up without meaning to, and I'd always found humor a good way to restore the mood. It worked.

Sage grinned and shook her head. "You got that right."

I topped off her wine. "I'll say no more, but will you do me one small favor?"

She studied me suspiciously. "What?"

"If you ever change your mind, or you find yourself in a tight spot that I can easily help with, will you come to me?"

"Elliot." She sighed heavily.

"Please."

"Okay, but just know it's very unlikely to happen."

I chuckled. "Goddamn proud woman."

"You'd better believe it. Now, let's finish this meal and get to work."

———

Sage flopped against the stack of cushions lined up along one wall of what I'd dubbed 'The Evidence Room' and pinched the bridge of her nose, a deeply resigned sigh spilling out of her.

"There's nothing, Elliot. Damn, I wanted to find something, but whoever did this is extremely good at covering their tracks."

I palmed the back of my neck where it ached from the last few hours bent over studying every scrap of information gathered over four years. "Let's take a break."

I went to join her, lying on my side, my elbow propping up my head. Her T-shirt had ridden up slightly, offering a glimpse of the dip of her waist. I traced the soft skin with my fingertip. She shuffled out of my reach, then got to her feet.

"Don't."

I sat up and crossed my legs, studying her flushed cheeks and perky nipples that begged for my tongue. Whatever her reasons for rejecting me, they didn't include lack of desire.

"Why?"

Appearing exasperated, she swept a hand over her face. "We've had this conversation. It isn't a good idea."

"Why?"

My questioning style was an applied technique in business. Keep asking why until you got to the heart of the issue. Eventually, the truth would reveal itself.

"I've told you. I'm not interested in a one-night stand with a man who is clearly on the rebound."

"Who said anything about a one-night stand?" I decided to ignore, for now, her point about being on the rebound. The evidence showed that no matter how many times I reassured her that wasn't the case, she appeared determined to believe it.

"You did." She kicked out her hip and raised her eyes up and to the right. "What was it you said? 'All those years of pent-up frustration unleashed in a single night of rampant passion'. Be honest, Elliot. All you're really interested in is a quick fuck with a girl who mooned after you in high school to help you prove you're over a long-term relationship that ended badly."

I might not have seen Sage for many years, but I'd bet this house and a large part of my fortune that her irritated outburst had nothing to do with me and my persistent sexual advances, and everything to do with her frustration at the lack of progress on uncovering who'd taken Athena.

When she'd agreed to help, in her mind she'd thought finding the perp would be a shoo-in, and she'd emerge triumphant with the answer. I mean, a professional law enforcement officer had to stand a better chance of solving a crime than a billionaire executive, right?

Wrong.

There wasn't a fucker on the planet more determined than me, or more diligent at combing through reams of data to arrive at a conclusion. Okay, maybe Garen could best me on the data stuff, but I wasn't far behind.

"That's a hell of a memory," I teased. "Those words must've meant something. And just so we're clear, I'm not interested in a one-night stand. All I meant was that our first night together would be explosive."

She snorted, and it was so cute on her, I couldn't help but smile, which seemed to annoy her even further.

"Laugh all you like, Elliot, but I'm not interested in sleeping with you."

"Why?"

She growled and slammed her fists into her thighs. "You are so irritating."

"Only because I'm asking questions that, for some reason, you won't answer. All these bullshit excuses. Why don't you tell me what the real problem is, Sage? And don't insult my intelligence by refusing to admit you're attracted to me."

"Fine," she spat. "I'm attracted to you. I fancied the hell out of you at high school, and fuck me, you've improved with age. But this obsession with finding the man who abducted your sister scares me, Elliot. You're so resolute that you're willing to risk everything—your girlfriend, your friends, your livelihood—in order to chase shadows. Persistence is an admirable trait, but not to the detriment of other, more important things. You've already lost so much, yet you barely stopped to draw breath before pushing on and leaving a trail of destruction in your wake. You're on a road to nowhere with this pointless search, yet still you press ahead, refusing to admit the fruitlessness of it all. And if I allow myself to become embroiled in the net you've cast, I'm scared I'll drown right along with you."

The words *you don't understand* were on the tip of my tongue, but just in time, I swallowed them. If anyone knew the burning need to avenge a loved one, it was the woman standing in front of me, and to say otherwise not only disrespected her but would likely mean I never saw her again. Sage needed reassurance, not accusations.

"I admit that when I want something, I pursue it relentlessly, and I'm rarely knocked off course until I achieve my aim. But when you agreed to help me, you set out a warning and a condition, and I heard them, loud and clear."

"Did you?" she asked, her voice so quiet that I leaned forward to better hear her. "It's over, Elliot. There's nothing here. It's hopeless, and to pretend otherwise is crazy. For your sanity, you need to face up to the fact that we don't always get what we want or what we deserve. Bad people do bad things, and sometimes they don't pay for them. It's time to put this behind you and move on with your life."

"Not a fucking chance." I sprang to my feet and shoved my hands into my pockets, then immediately removed them and jabbed a finger at her as the red mist descended. "You gave up on your sister. I refuse to give up on mine."

"How dare you?" A rash of color mottled her neck and chest. "This is exactly what I'm talking about. You've lost the ability to rationalize, to look at the problem logically and assess the chances of success. It's over, Elliot."

"It's over when *I* say it's over," I ground out, barely holding on to my burgeoning temper. "Four years I've been at this. Four fucking years, and you don't see me giving up. Yet one month in and you've flaked on me. You promised me three months, Sage. Then again, I bet you promised your sister you'd find the man who wrecked her life, too."

Her jaw scissored from side to side, and her nostrils flared. "That's it. I'm leaving."

She wrenched open the door.

I gripped her upper arm. "Wait."

She coldly stared at my fingers wrapped around her biceps and then jutted her chin upwards. "Take your hand off me or I swear to God, Elliot, you'll lose it."

I immediately released her and raked a hand through my hair, clarity appearing with startling horror. "I'm sorry. Fuck, I'm really sorry. I don't want you to go. I'm just..." I spun around and hung my head.

When I turned back around, she'd gone.

Chapter Eleven

SAGE

My cell phone dinged with a text. I glanced at it and immediately deleted the message without reading it. I didn't have to open it to know what it'd say, or at least the general idea. Over the past four and a half weeks, I'd received a gazillion of them, each one in a similar vein.

I'm sorry. Forgive me. I didn't mean it. Please call me back.

I'd considered changing my number, but it was so damned inconvenient these days. So many people to get around to giving the new one to. I didn't have the energy. Same went for my email. At least with that, I could set up a rule that immediately deleted any emails from Elliot. I suppose I could block his number—and I hadn't yet quite figured out why I failed to take that final step.

For the first few days after I'd walked out on him, he'd turned up at the precinct at the start of every shift. I'd refused to speak to him and, eventually, I'd sent Beth down to threaten to arrest him for stalking if he didn't quit coming around here. That seemed to do the trick regarding physical visits, but technology provided a way for him to continue badgering me and begging for forgiveness.

His words had stung, especially those aimed at Lily. Then again, I'd hit the mark with a few of my own comments, albeit I hadn't shouted mine in anger. Didn't make them any less painful. And on reflection, I could see Elliot's point of view that he thought I'd flaked on him. Given he'd spent four years searching for the man who'd hurt his sister, I understood why he might think my giving up after a month meant I hadn't put the effort in. What he failed to acknowledge was my vast years of experience in the police force. I knew a dead end when I saw one, and sadly, I'd seen my fair share of them. If I had a dime for every family who'd had to accept the lack of justice in their case, I'd have a far healthier bank balance.

"Sage."

I glanced over my shoulder to find Beth with her head poked around the door.

"Me and a few of the team are heading over to Finnegan's for a 'thank fuck it's Friday' drink. Want to join?"

I wasn't really in the mood, and I'd already blown off Cassandra when she'd called earlier in the day with a suggestion of maybe meeting halfway between New York and her place upstate for a catch-up. I'd hardly seen Beth, given our conflicting work schedules, but at least with her, I'd find it easy to escape after one drink. With Cass, her version of a catch-up would soon turn into a madness-and-mayhem evening, and I'd spend my weekend off recovering from a killer hangover.

"Sure. Just finishing up a few things. I'll follow you over."

"Great. I'll get the first round in."

I gestured an acknowledgement, then began closing the files on my desk. I stood, stretching out my back, and wandered over to the filing cabinet to put them away. My desk phone rang. I groaned and almost ignored it. I was off the clock so under no obligation to answer, but the committed cop in me lifted the receiver anyway.

"Abbott."

"Oh, hi. Is that Sage Abbott?"

"Yeah, who's this?"

"My name is Diana Jones. I'm the operations manager at the Foxhill Retreat Center here in Scottsdale. You submitted an application a few months ago for your sister, Lily, to come to stay with us on a short break. I'm thrilled to say that we've had a last-minute cancellation for March twenty-sixth for two weeks. I hope that time fits in with your schedule."

Oh God. I'd completely forgotten about that application, and knowing the acceptance criteria as well as how popular it was, I hadn't thought for one second that I'd ever receive an invitation. Foxhill was a retreat for adults with mental health challenges. They were seen as world-class in providing a stimulating and supportive environment and offered both residential and short-break stays. When I'd filled in the online forms, Mom had been at a particularly low ebb— caring for Lily wasn't easy on either of us, but Mom felt it more deeply than I did. Lily was her child, after all. I'd desperately wanted to give her a break, so I'd rashly filled in the online form and then promptly forgotten all about it. I'd put my work number on the form so that, in the unlikely event they called, there wouldn't be a risk of catching me at home. I hadn't told Mom about the application, partly because I didn't want to get her hopes up.

"Miss Abbott? Are you still there?"

"Yes, sorry. Erm, that's... that's great."

My hesitation must have filtered down the line because she asked, "Are you still interested in having Lily stay with us? We have a rather long waiting list, as I'm sure you can imagine."

Time to face the thorny issue of money. When I'd applied for a place, the price hadn't been on the website, and as I'd felt so certain they'd never offer me one, I hadn't contacted them to ask.

"Um, how much is it?"

"The fully inclusive cost for the entire stay is fifteen thousand dollars."

My heart felt like it was shrinking, and a band tightened around my chest. There was no way I could afford even a tenth of that. We lived paycheck to paycheck. Someone always had to be there to take care of Lily, and so Mom had a casual gig at a local grocery store where she sometimes worked on the days or nights I wasn't on shift. I never should have applied. Now that they had offered me a place, all I wanted was for Lily to have the opportunity to go, and yet I'd let her down.

"When do you need to know by?"

She paused, and an image of her rolling her eyes and thinking 'waste of time' flashed before me.

"I can give you until this time tomorrow, but I'm afraid if you can't confirm by then, we'll have to offer the place to the next person on the waiting list."

I rarely cried. My job didn't allow for such displays of emotion, but the burn of hot tears stung behind my eyelids, and I blinked several times to clear my vision.

"I understand. I'll call you tomorrow. You have my word."

"Thank you. Have a good night."

She hung up, and I let my head drop at the sheer hopelessness of it all.

I lost track of how long I sat there, but the buzzing of my phone jerked me from contemplation. I glanced at the screen. Beth. No doubt she'd called to find out where on earth I'd gotten to. I let it ring out, then dropped her a text.

Need to bail. Something's come up. Sorry.

I followed up with another text to Mom. She wasn't expecting me home at any particular time tonight, but I always shot her a message if I planned to go anywhere after my shift ended. I needed time to think and run some figures I already knew wouldn't yield the right result, but that wouldn't stop me from trying.

A chill wind curled around my neck as I exited the precinct, and I pulled up the collar on my coat and bent my head. Powering through the throngs of people either heading home following a long work week, or maybe starting their weekend early, I ducked into my favorite deli and grabbed a seat by the window. My stomach rumbled. I hadn't eaten since breakfast. I ordered a pastrami on wheat and a coffee. Using a napkin as a jotting pad, I began noting down ideas, but by the time my sandwich and drink arrived, I was no closer to an answer.

Fifteen thousand dollars. It might as well be fifteen million dollars. Even if I maxed out my credit card, it wouldn't come close, and given I had no assets to offer as collateral, a bank loan was out of the question. Banks didn't lend to people like me. They lent to people who could afford to pay the installments.

Oh God, it's hopeless.

But this break was just the thing Mom needed. People often misunderstood the stress on those who cared for others. I had it easy compared to Mom. Out of the two of us, she spent far more time with Lily than I did, and lately she'd looked so tired and worn down for someone her age. She was only fifty-five, yet to a stranger, she appeared at least ten years older than that.

Come on, Sage. Think.

Maybe I could start a fundraiser. The guys at work would chip in. But as fast as that idea came to me, I discarded it. I had to confirm by tomorrow that I had the money to pay for Lily's place. A fundraiser would take weeks to set up, and there wasn't time to organize it.

I tore the napkin with the useless numbers jotted down into tiny pieces of confetti. It didn't matter how hard Mom and I worked, we just seemed to stand still, never able to move forward. Not for the first time, it occurred to me that I'd made a mistake in remaining at the rank of officer. I should have pushed for promotion. Gone down the detective route, or, like Beth, followed the chain of command up to captain, major, or even beyond. That wasn't me, though. I enjoyed being out on the streets, working directly with the residents of this city that I loved. Promotions further up the tree resulted in incessant meetings and piles of paperwork, leaving much less time for what I thought of as community policing.

Besides, all this pointless musing wouldn't help with my current dilemma.

And then a lightbulb went off. Well, not so much a lightbulb as a thunderclap. *Elliot.* Before we'd had our falling out, he'd made me promise that if I ever needed anything, I'd go to him.

No.

I couldn't do it. Not given the way we'd left things, and how I'd ignored every olive branch he'd extended for the past few weeks. We'd both said things we probably shouldn't have, or at least should have remained calm when saying them, but to go cap in hand with my begging bowl extended to ask Elliot to help Lily when he didn't even know her was a step too far for my pride to take.

Then again, this wasn't about me. It was about Lily.

I let my head fall into my hands. *Fuck.*

I'd do it. I'd do it for Lily. For Mom.

And if he slams the door in your face?

I hoped it wouldn't come to that.

Chapter Twelve

ELLIOT

SAGE MUST HAVE BLOCKED MY NUMBER AND MY email address. Not that I blamed her. If I were in her shoes, I'd have done exactly the same. To rail on her like I had was unforgiveable. I'd thought of nothing else in the last few weeks, and it was driving me crazy. All I wanted was to spend five minutes with her so I could unreservedly apologize, but she'd denied me that, and it was all my own damned fault.

At one time I'd have said my reaction to her was completely out of character. Not these days. My moods switched on a dime, and anger boiled up out of nowhere, and I'd unleash it on my nearest and dearest. Mom, Athena, Ryker, Dad. None of them escaped my rage. No wonder they kept me at arm's length.

The past few years had taken their toll, but giving up wasn't an option. At the age of eight, I'd vowed to protect my sister and my mother, and on this occasion, I'd failed Athena. That fucker had snatched her right off the street in broad daylight, and there hadn't been a damn thing I could've done to stop him.

Tracking him down and making him pay for his crimes was the only thing keeping me sane, yet at the same time, I teetered on the edge of an insanity brought about by an unwavering search for the truth, one that was slowly alienating everyone around me. Sage had been right about that. I just didn't want to admit it, and when she'd bluntly pointed it out, I'd laid the full force of my wrath at her door.

I felt so alone, and yet when Sage had offered to help me, for the first time in a very long while, I wasn't. And I'd loved spending time with her. Hence when she'd told me it was over, all I'd seen was that loneliness opening up once more, like a black chasm that threatened to swallow me, and it had clouded my judgement.

I groaned aloud as I thought of how I'd gripped her arm. Not painfully. I'd only wanted her to stay, but my intentions didn't matter one iota. While angry, I'd put my hands on a woman. Violence toward women was a trigger for me, and that one simple act had sparked a cacophony of dreadful thoughts that I wasn't any different from the man who created me. No wonder I hadn't slept a wink since.

You're losing it, man.

I wandered from room to room. I hated this house. It'd been Brie's choice. I'd rather live uptown in an apartment overlooking Central Park. Hmm. Nothing stopping me now. I snatched up my phone and began looking up realtors. I made a few notes and vowed to call them tomorrow. The Manhattan property market moved fast. With any luck, I could be out of here in a couple of months.

A tentative knock at the door drew my eyebrows into a frown. I wasn't expecting anyone. I strode to the front door and opened it. My heart nigh on stopped, and joy mingled with concern filled my chest.

"Sage?"

She jutted up her chin and combined the assertive stance with a wry smile. "Is this a bad time?"

"No. Not at all. Come in, please."

I stood back to let her enter, careful to give her space. The shock of her turning up out of the blue after ghosting me for weeks had left me a little off-balance.

"Can I take your coat?"

"Um, sure."

She shrugged out of it, and I hung it in the closet. I couldn't stop my eyes from wandering over her face, her body. God, I'd missed her.

"Can I get you a drink? Wine, beer, a cocktail?" I grinned, hoping a smile might take the edge off the atmosphere.

"A glass of water would be great."

Water. Okay, then.

I walked through to the kitchen with Sage following me and grabbed a bottle of mineral water and a beer from the fridge. "Ice?"

She shook her head. I poured the water into a glass and handed it to her.

"Thanks."

She sipped, then set it on the kitchen island. I twisted the bottle cap off the beer and took aim at the trash can in the corner—and missed. I didn't surprise me. Screwing up was the story of my life at the moment.

"I wasn't sure you'd be in. You know. Friday night and all."

"I'm kinda lacking in people willing to put up with me, so it's just me on my lonesome." I pulled a cartoon-sad face, hoping to make her laugh. It did.

"You only have yourself to blame for that."

Determined to keep it light despite the heaviness weighing on my shoulders as it often did these days, I pressed a hand to my chest. "You wound me. Here I am, lying on the floor, and you're kicking me while I'm already down."

"It's the cop in me."

She shuffled, shooting me the odd look, but mostly focusing her attention on the condensation dripping down the side of her glass. She caught a droplet with her finger and brought it to her mouth. I groaned. She heard. Her eyes met mine.

"How have you been?" she asked.

"Lonely."

Her face twisted, and I didn't like it, so I added, "Horny," and hit her with a mischievous grin.

"You don't give up, do you?"

"Never."

She sighed heavily. "You hurt me, Elliot. Those things you said about Lily. I didn't simply give up on finding the man who assaulted my sister. I accepted that sometimes it doesn't matter how much we want something, or how hard we strive for it, we will ultimately end up disappointed. Life sucks. It kills me that the man who ruined her life is still out there. But there came a time when the only sensible and logical thing to do was to let it go. Lily deserved all of me, not this revenge-fueled woman who spent every spare moment chasing a ghost while leaving Mom to pick up the pieces."

Her not-so-hidden correlation with my own life hit its mark, but I wasn't Sage. She was a far better person than I was. I couldn't let go, to admit to myself—and to Athena—that the bastard who'd taken her had gotten away with it.

"I shouldn't have said those things, but you didn't exactly hold back with your views either."

"Because I know where it leads," she said, a tinge of exasperation raising the tone of her voice. She took a deep breath and pinched her nose. "If you're not careful, you'll lose everything. Rock bottom isn't a place you want to visit. I've seen so many people in similar positions to you where their loved ones were murdered, or raped, or kidnapped and tortured, and those who can't accept and move on end up in a very dark place. I don't want that for you. We live in a cruel world, and sometimes, the bad guys don't get what they deserve."

"You promised three months. You reneged on that promise. How did you expect me to react?"

"I said I'd give it three months before I'd looked at a scrap of evidence, and I shouldn't have. I'm an experienced law enforcement officer, not some wet-behind-the-ears rookie straight from the academy. If there was even a slim lead, I promise you, I'd have found it. But there's nothing there. Whoever did this is long gone. I'm not saying never. There is always hope. Cold cases sometimes spring back to life in ways that surprise us, but I am begging you not to let this consume your life any more than it already has."

I swigged my beer, then set it down beside her glass and traced the back of her hand with my pinky, buoyed when she didn't pull away. "I'm glad you came back," I said, my voice deep and husky, and filled with a growing lust for the woman standing close enough for me to kiss.

"I didn't come here to tell you I'd changed my mind about the case. I haven't."

I flexed my jaw, my eyes narrowing as I glared down at her. "Then why are you here?"

She breathed heavily through her nose and slowly blinked. "I need a favor. It's a big one, and I wouldn't be here if I had any other choice."

I snort-laughed. "Nice. FYI, you suck at negotiation."

"That came out wrong."

She touched my arm, and my skin heated from her touch. I stared at the connection, wanting more. *Needing* more. But she either misread the signals or she decided she'd made a mistake because she drew back.

"It's not for me. It's for Lily."

That got my attention. I'd never met Sage's sister, but her story touched me deeply. Life had dealt her a shitty hand, and if I had it in my power to help in any way, I'd jump at the chance. Besides, it'd get me back in Sage's good books, and I'd do almost anything to slide back between those pages.

I had to stop with the sexual innuendos running through my head. I was already frustrated. My dick did not need any further help.

"What do you need?"

She nibbled her lip. I'd never seen Sage so uncomfortable, and that included our time together in high school when she constantly looked out of place.

I tucked a lock of hair behind her ear, taking encouragement when she expelled a brief hiss. "Ask me, Sage," I rasped.

"Fifteen thousand dollars." She blushed fiercely, her cheeks blotchy with embarrassment. "I need a loan for fifteen thousand dollars."

I doubted Sage Abbott had ever asked anyone for a dime in her entire life. She reeked of self-reliance. I bet she thought asking for help was a weakness, a heinous crime against her determination to make it alone.

How wrong she was.

"What's the money for?"

She wrapped her arms around herself, and I almost asked if she was cold, despite the warmth in the house, but then I realized it was a form of protection.

"Ages ago, I applied for Lily to take a short break at this retreat down in Arizona. They specialize in her kind of challenges, and Mom so desperately needs a brief respite. I honestly never thought they'd offer me a place. It's a highly sought-after establishment. Today, as I was leaving work, they called and said they'd had a cancellation for a week from Tuesday for a two-week stay. I have until tomorrow to find the money or they'll release the place to someone else."

The desolation in her eyes punched me in the gut. My response came easy.

"The money's yours. On two conditions."

Relief hit her so hard, she didn't even hesitate, just said, "Fine. Name your price."

Rookie mistake. Never agree to anything until you know what your opponent is asking for.

"First, I want an apology."

Her eyebrows disappeared behind her bangs. "An apology? For what?"

"For breaking your word."

"I've already explained that."

"I know."

She rolled her eyes and crossed her arms over her chest. "Okay. I'm sorry about that, but I'm not sorry for the things I said either then or tonight. I stand by every word."

Damn, that fire in her eyes went straight to my dick. She really was glorious. All that contained passion locked up tight. And no matter what it took, I'd find the key.

"And the second condition?" she asked.

Distracted, I blinked. "You stick out the full three months you originally agreed to."

She expelled an exasperated sigh. "Elliot..."

I held up my hands. "That's the deal. Take it or leave it."

The money for Lily was hers, whether she agreed or she didn't. But she deserved a little payback for throwing in the towel, and I was enjoying myself far too much to stop now.

She rummaged around in her coat and produced her phone, then swiped the screen and tapped on it.

"What are you doing?" I asked, wondering if she'd decided to call the cops on my ass. For what, I wasn't sure, but the silence unnerved me.

"I'm adding a note to my calendar for exactly two months from now. May fifteenth. It says, and I quote, 'Elliot's extortion ends.'"

I chuckled. "You're magnificent. You know that?"

"And you're taking a hell of a risk blackmailing a cop."

"It's not blackmail, Sage, just a bit of a... friendly nudge in the right direction."

She snorted. God, I adored her.

"Shall I email over my banking details?"

"Yeah. I'll wire the money right away."

She gave me the softest smile, and my dick punched against my zipper.

"Thank you. You have no idea what this means. I can't wait to tell Mom and Lily."

She made a move to leave. I snagged her around the waist, pulling her into my body. She'd definitely feel my hard-on, but it wasn't like it'd come as a surprise. She knew how badly I wanted her. I'd told her often enough.

"Don't go."

Her lips parted, and they were so close. So damned close. I leaned in. She pressed a hand to my chest.

"Elliot, I just... I... it's not a good—"

My mouth cut her off before she could finish her sentence. I palmed her lower back and ground into her. Stiffness lingered in her body, but then she relaxed and melted into me, her fingers weaving into the hair at my nape. She smelled of lemons and peaches and an enduring trace of perfume that she'd probably dabbed on her neck earlier this morning. My heart pounded, forcing blood into my veins, and resulting in a dick stretched so tight, I feared the skin might burst.

"God, Sage." I breathed her name, feathering my lips over her jawline, down the exquisite curve of her neck. I returned to her lips, capturing them once more. I walked her backward until her spine butted up against a flat wall to the left of the doorway. Lightly, I trailed my fingertips up her sides, hovering at the swell of her tits. I'd give a limb to bury my head between them, or better still, my dick.

She tugged hard on my hair, sending a burn through my scalp, but I couldn't give a shit. She could yank it out at the roots as long as she kept rubbing her scorching-hot body against me like that and making those sounds of pleasure that I wanted to record so I could get myself off to them whenever I wanted.

"Let's go upstairs."

She stilled, then slowly tipped back her head, her eyes catching mine. "I'm not sure that's such a good idea."

"I think it's a marvelous idea."

She giggled, as I'd hoped she would. "Why doesn't that surprise me?"

"Because I'm a man, and I'm horny, and slipping

between the sheets with a beautiful woman is *always* a good idea."

"Unfortunately for you, I'm a woman whose DNA is entrenched in taking things a tad slower."

"Damn genetics."

She cradled my face, and I leaned in like a cat seeking affection from its owner. That wasn't too far from the truth. I wanted affection. The woman fucking owned me.

"Can I see you again tomorrow?"

"I'm working the night shift through next Wednesday. I'll call you, though."

I tried to hide my disappointment, kissing her gently. "Be careful out there on the streets."

She laughed. "I can take care of myself. You should see me take a two hundred and fifty pound hunk of beef to the ground."

"How about tackling a one-eighty guy to the mattress? I'll even let you handcuff me."

She snickered. "Ten points for persistence."

I threw my arms out to the sides. "Angel, it's me. You wouldn't expect anything else, surely?"

Her eyes narrowed, and she wagged her finger at me, reminding me of a parent scolding a child. "I can see I'm going to have trouble with you."

I fake shuddered. "And it'll be so much fun."

Chapter Thirteen

SAGE

CALLING DIANA JONES THE FOLLOWING DAY AND confirming the place for Lily put a smile on my face that nothing could shift. Elliot had stuck to his word and wired the funds right into my bank account, which I could then send on to Foxhill. As soon as the administration was out of the way, I sat Mom and Lily down to share the good news.

Mom burst into tears—which only added to the mounting evidence that this was a break she so desperately needed. Lily squealed and jumped up and down, especially at the part where I told her they had horses that she'd be able to learn to ride. Lily loved all animals, but dogs and horses were her favorites. I wished we lived in a place that allowed pets, but our renters agreement didn't consent to a fish tank, let alone a domestic animal.

Dreams kept me going that one day, I'd save enough money to buy a small house with a yard. Those dreams might be of the pipe variety, but that didn't stop me imagining a time when it might happen. If I ever achieved that goal, the first item on the list would be a puppy for my sister.

Lily burned herself out with all the excitement, so Mom put her down for a nap. Once she reappeared in the living room, I took one look at her face and prepped myself for the third degree.

"How much is this place, Sage?"

I waved dismissively. "That's not something you need to worry about."

"Except I *am* worried. A facility like that must have cost an absolute fortune. How have you afforded the fees? Please tell me you didn't go to a loan shark."

I suppressed a chuckle and made a mental note to tell Elliot my mother thought him a loan shark. "No, Mom. I didn't. A friend helped me out."

Her frown deepened. "What kind of friend doles out thousands of dollars? And what do they want in return?"

"He's an old high school friend."

That description stretched the truth a bit, but it was for Mom's benefit. She didn't need to know I hadn't seen Elliot in a very long time, and we'd never actually been friends in school.

"He's done well for himself and he wanted to help me out, that's all. No strings attached."

Another lie. Elliot had definitely attached strings.

She picked up my hand and tenderly stroked the back. "Sage, honey, where men are concerned, there are *always* strings."

I laughed. "He's nice, Mom. You'd like him."

"Is that so? In that case, you should invite him for dinner. That way I can make up my own mind."

Oh shit. Foot. Mouth. Crap all over the place.

"Um, I wasn't planning to invite him to come here. He's a busy man. He runs a large international company." *That he's currently on the bench from and therefore has more time on his hands than he knows what to do with.*

"I won't hear of it, Sage," Mom pressed. "The least we can do is make the boy a home-cooked meal to thank him for his generosity."

I snorted. Mom didn't fool me. She wanted to interrogate Elliot until she'd satisfied herself he wouldn't lead me astray. I clung to the silver lining that he'd politely decline, making some excuse or other. I wasn't stupid. All Elliot wanted was my help to find his sister's abductor, and to get me into bed. Once he'd achieved both goals, he'd disappear from my life. We moved in completely different circles. Longevity wasn't in the cards here.

A lump of regret settled in my stomach, but before I could dwell on it, Mom nudged me.

"Well?"

I sighed, acknowledging there was little point in continuing the argument. "Fine, I'll ask him, but if our schedules don't line up, can you drop it, please? I'll have to work extra shifts to make up for the time off I'll need to take Lily down to Arizona and settle her in, so I don't have many free nights between now and then."

Mom patted my upper arm. "You'll figure it out."

———

I wasn't sure whether Elliot agreeing—enthusiastically, I might add—to an invitation to dinner was a good or a bad thing. My instincts said bad. Elliot was unpredictable at the best of times, and I never knew what might come out of his mouth. The last thing I wanted was for Mom to find out we'd played one or two games of tonsil hockey. I'd prefer to stick to the 'just friends' moniker, but I wouldn't put it past Elliot to slide the odd comment in there that'd give Mom cause to grill me once he left.

He arrived right on time loaded down with a huge bouquet of flowers, a box of chocolates, and a giant cuddly toy. I could barely see him behind the armfuls of gifts.

"You are such a cliché," I said.

"They're not for you," he replied, a twinkle in his eye. "The teddy bear is for Lily, and the flowers and chocolates are for your mom to thank her for inviting me over."

"Oh." I nibbled my lip and tried to stem the approaching embarrassed blush.

"Don't worry, Sage," he murmured in my ear. "I have a much better gift for you."

His voice dripped sex. A whole swarm of butterflies took flight in my stomach, their wings flapping against my insides. I rolled my eyes to hide the effect his words had on me and spat out a sarcastic response. "Really? And what's that? The python in your trousers?"

He grinned broadly. "Python, huh? I'll take it."

Irritated, I huffed. "There's no talking to you."

I spun on my heel, the low rumble of his laugh following me.

"Mom, this is Elliot Bancroft. He's brought bribes... I mean gifts."

Elliot sniggered again, then expertly shifted the presents around to allow him to shake Mom's outstretched hand.

"Thank you for inviting me, Mrs. Abbott. These are for you." He handed over the flowers and chocolates.

"Oh, they're lovely," Mom said, burying her nose in the blooms and taking a big sniff. "They smell divine. How thoughtful." Her gaze went to the giant bear Elliot had moved to his hip, much as one would hold a child. She clasped a hand to her chest. "Is that for Lily?"

Elliot nodded. "It sure is."

Mom's chin wobbled, and I could have sworn she made gooey eyes at Elliot. "She'll love it."

I spotted Elliot glancing around, and I guessed at his query. "Lily's not feeling very well. She's sleeping."

"Oh, that's a shame. Nothing too serious?"

"Just a little bug, I think," Mom replied. "She'll bounce back in no time. Now, come sit down, Elliot. I want to know everything."

My shoulders sagged. A long evening lay ahead.

Two hours later, and I had to admit Elliot had this whole 'handling the parents' thing mastered. It made me wonder how much practice he'd had. Not as much in the last few years, I'd guess, given the long-term nature of his previous relationship, but he had my mother entranced, and for a naturally suspicious woman, that was quite a feat.

Then again, he wasn't here as my boyfriend, which probably made it easier. Less pressure to impress.

I ignored the prickle of regret that thought engendered and refilled his glass with Mom's special homemade lemonade. The smile he shot me, combined with the way he surreptitiously stroked up the inside of my thigh beneath the table, almost caused me to spontaneously combust. I launched to my feet and began clearing away the empty plates.

"Dessert?"

My voice sounded weird enough that Mom gave me an odd look. Elliot merely grinned. He knew exactly the effect that sneaky leg caress had on me.

"You sit down. I'll do it," she said.

"No, it's okay, Mom. You cooked."

I picked up the stack and ducked into the kitchen. Thank God this apartment wasn't open plan. I almost dropped the plates in the sink, then braced myself against the counter and stared through the window into the dark night. I'd tried to ignore the mounting attraction I felt toward Elliot, yet despite my best efforts, it'd grown into something huge, larger than the stuffed bear he'd brought as a gift for Lily. Then again, it'd only been a matter of time before his not-so-hidden sexual innuendos and blatant advances were impossible to resist. If Cass were here, I knew exactly what she'd say, which was the precise reason I hadn't mentioned Elliot to her, brushing off the night of her birthday celebrations as a one-off, never-to-be-repeated chance encounter with an old school friend. Lucky for me, Cass didn't have a long attention span, and had soon forgotten Elliot's brief appearance.

If only it was that simple for me.

Oh, screw it. If I didn't have sex soon, my vagina would put up a No Entry sign. So what if the little niggle about Elliot's ex wouldn't let up? He'd reassured me enough times that he was over it, hardly giving her a second thought. Maybe the time had come to believe him. A few nights of passionate sex might be just what the sex therapist ordered. Not that I'd ever visited a sex therapist.

Maybe I should visit a sex therapist.

FFS! Get a grip, Sage.

Four years, though. Such a long time to be with someone and then claim to feel no aftereffects when they were no longer in the picture.

"I like your Mom."

I spun around and banged my elbow on the side of the fridge. "Ow." I gave it a rub.

"Oh, poor angel."

Elliot pushed off the doorjamb where he'd loitered, watching me for God only knew how long, and prowled farther into the kitchen.

"Want me to kiss it better?"

"Elliot, stop," I hissed, shooting a quick glance over his shoulder into the living room. I'd convinced Mom—or at least I thought I had—that Elliot was exactly what I'd professed him to be. A friend. Nothing more. It would ruin all my hard work if she overheard him talking about kissing and calling me angel.

"She's gone to check on Lily," Elliot explained with one more step that brought him close enough that I could smell his bodywash and the merest trace of a musky cologne. I breathed in. He smelled so good.

Gently circling my wrist, his fingers long and tanned with perfectly shaped nails, he tugged. I almost fell against his chest and I put out a hand to steady myself. Big mistake. Elliot Bancroft worked out. Either that, or he was some kind of superhuman gifted with strong, hard pecs without lifting a barbell at the gym. Whatever the reason, I wasn't complaining.

"Did you just moan?"

I jolted back to the present and out of my head, which I'd begun to realize wasn't a safe place for me to be. Not if I was making inadvertent sex sounds.

"Don't be silly."

I tried to put some space between us. Elliot was having none of it. In fact, he shifted his weight, bringing us even closer together.

"I think you did."

He bound me in his arms and traced the tip of his nose over mine. *Christ...* Why was that so sexy? I held my breath. That way I couldn't talk, or moan, or make any kind of encouraging noise.

"Come home with me tonight and I'll make you do more than moan."

"Sage, Lily wants to... oh."

I twisted out of Elliot's grasp and met my mother's surprised gaze as she bounced between me and Elliot. *Goddamn.*

"So sorry to interrupt, kids."

She giggled. I glared, partly for the interruption, and partly for calling us kids.

"You almost had me convinced, Sage, although why you seem hell-bent on hiding the fact you're in a relationship is beyond me."

"We're not in a relationship," I insisted, looking to Elliot for backup. I didn't get any. Instead, he hung me out to dry.

"The truth, Mrs. Abbott, is that I had a rather large crush on Sage in high school but, as you do, we lost touch. And then, fortuitously, she came back into my life and, well, it's made both of us extremely happy, hasn't it, angel?" He didn't wait for a response before crashing on. "It's all very new, and although I'd love to shout it from the rooftops, Sage would like to keep things on the down low for a while, and of course, I want to respect her wishes."

While my tongue flapped, virtually useless at forming any kind of intelligible words, Mom's smile almost split her face wide open.

"I'm thrilled for you, darling. It's about time you had a life of your own. You've been such a support to me since

Lily's accident, but you shouldn't give up your life for me or for Lily."

"She's very committed," Elliot continued. "Both to her job and to you and Lily. As she should be. Family is very important. My sister means the world to me, so I know exactly how Sage feels about Lily."

He pecked my cheek. I clenched my fists. As soon as Mom left us alone, one of them was going to connect with his too-handsome face. What I couldn't quite figure out was why he wanted Mom to think we were in a relationship. We weren't. Far from it.

"It's just a shame we don't get to spend as much time together as I'd like."

I went to speak. It came out as little more than a squeaking noise that resembled a mouse when I'd aimed for the roar of a lion. What the hell was he playing at?

And then, right when I thought things couldn't get any worse, Mom excitedly clapped her hands.

"Well then, that settles it. You should go with Sage and Lily to Arizona."

Chapter Fourteen

ELLIOT

I ALMOST CHOKED, SWALLOWING THE LAUGH THAT threatened to burst out of me at Sage's astounded expression. All night she'd heavily hinted that we were barely even friends and my offer of financial help had only come about because we'd attended high school together—leaving out the part where we'd moved in different circles and only ever lusted after each other from afar—and as I had more money than the GDP of some small countries, I'd wanted to help.

I'd felt it was more than time for a little payback of my own. Alluding to her mom that Sage and I were far closer than she'd made out was the most fun I'd had in ages. She wasn't exactly going to call me a liar in front of her mother. That would only raise more questions, ones she wouldn't want to answer.

Besides, inducing an impromptu invite to Arizona played right into my hands. Time alone with Sage? Yes, please. She'd hardly be able to avoid me—and of course I'd offer to take care of the hotel reservations so we could be close by to help Lily settle in for a couple days. The penthouse suite at the ROGUES Scottsdale hotel would do very nicely. Three bedrooms—even if I planned to only use one—a private pool on the roof, and a glorious mountain view. Yep. Done deal.

"That's a wonderful idea, Mrs. Abbott," I said, taking further advantage of the situation while Sage still couldn't find her voice. I slung my arm around her shoulder and landed another kiss, this time in her hair.

Her mother sighed wistfully. Sage smiled, the kind that left the eyes flat and cold, and slipped her arm around my waist, then pinched me hard. I hissed, covering it up with a cough.

"It's like a fairy tale." Mrs. Abbot pressed a hand to her chest. "Finding each other again after all this time and falling in love."

"We're not in love," Sage spluttered. "We've only been on two dates."

"Three," I corrected. "You forgot the night we met. I count that as a date."

I came so close to adding, *especially as you put me in handcuffs,* but even I wasn't that brave. Instead, I dared her with my eyes to tell her mother what really happened that night. She abstained, instead faking a yawn, and glared at me with a simple message. *I'll kill you once we're alone.* I flashed a quick wink, my response clear. *Can't wait.*

"I'm kinda beat," Sage said. "And I have a long day tomorrow. I'll see you out."

She bustled off, and I got a tremendous view of her ass as she sashayed into the living room.

"Thank you for having me over for dinner, Mrs. Abbott, and for the suggestion about Arizona. I do hope I haven't taken a spot you would have liked."

"Not at all." She leaned in and stage-whispered, "I can't wait to spend some time by myself. Don't judge me."

I chuckled. "Never."

Sage took one look at me, fire shooting from her eyes, and wrenched the door open, then stomped outside. *Guess she's walking me to my car.* I followed, my smile so wide that my cheeks ached. By the time I exited the building, Sage was already outside, scanning the street for my car.

"Serves you right," she said. "Your car's been stolen. Hah! That's what you get for being a lying dog."

Ah, she thinks I drove here in the Aston. On this occasion, I'd driven over in the car my parents bought me when I graduated college that Mom insisted on hanging on to. The Aston had drawn far too much attention from the gangs of teenagers hanging around on the street corners, and I didn't want to risk my luck a second time.

I fished in my pocket and produced the key, then clicked the button, and the turn signals to a nondescript blue sedan flashed.

"Looks fine to me."

Her lips thinned, and her jaw scissored. "Hilarious. Where's the other one?"

"Tucked up in bed—where we should be."

"After that performance?" She kicked back her head toward her apartment building and snorted. "Would you like to tell me what that was all about?"

I moved closer. She remained where she was. *Hmm. Interesting.* "You started playing the game, angel. I simply joined in from a different angle."

She released an exasperated huffing sound. "I didn't tell my mother there was anything going on between us, because there *isn't*."

"Really? Let's test that theory, shall we?"

I whipped my hand around the back of her head and jerked her toward me, joining our mouths in a kiss meant to debunk her beliefs. Because there *was* something going on. More than something. The heat between us that she kept trying to douse flared, exploding into a show any passersby wouldn't forget in a hurry. A growl slash moan sounded low in her throat, a non-verbal message that I hadn't gotten away scot-free. A shudder ran through my body. *I sure hope not.*

By the time we broke apart, both of us struggled to catch our breath. Sage's chest heaved, and I shamelessly stared at her tits while slowing my breathing.

"You infuriate me."

I caught the note of irritation in her voice, but beneath that, a huskiness that she tried to conceal.

"Relationships without a good dose of wrath on both sides aren't worth shit. I'd rather I infuriated you than the alternative."

"Then I'd say you'd achieved your aim," she snapped.

"Christ, you're resplendent when angry. Come home with me."

"No! God, Elliot, you're like a broken record. Besides," she added, sounding a touch softer, "I have to work tomorrow."

"I guess I can wait until we're in Arizona."

She sighed deeply. Her head rolled back, and she looked at the starless sky. New York had far too much light bleed to see many stars, and tonight was no exception.

"You double down on tenacity, you know that?"

"Persistence is one of my best features."

"That's up for debate."

"Great. It'll give us something to discuss in bed. I like to talk after sex."

She huffed, spun on her heel, and walked up the path toward the entrance to her building. "Goodnight, Elliot."

I grinned and shouted, "Night, angel. I'll be in touch about Arizona."

She flipped me the bird behind her back, then disappeared. I hummed for the entire journey home.

Tuesday couldn't come quick enough.

———

ROGUES, the company I ran with my five best friends—or at least used to run—had taken up most of my time for the past twelve years ever since a gaming app we developed in college went viral, thrusting us into a business world we weren't in the slightest bit prepared for. Somehow the six of us muddled through that first crazy eighteen months where sleep came at a premium and spare time or hobbies were for other people. Once we found our feet, life got a little easier, but I often worked twelve to fourteen-hour days, mainly because I got off on the thrill of landing the next big deal or besting the competition.

Yet now, as I rattled around this stupidly big house, every day lasted a month, or that's what it felt like. Which was the primary reason for my almost childish excitement as Filan drove over the Brooklyn Bridge on our way to pick up Sage and Lily for our trip to Arizona. The plane was fueled and waiting at a private airfield a few miles from La Guardia. I hadn't mentioned to Sage that we'd be flying down in my jet. I hoped it thrilled her rather than resulted in dismay at the ostentatious display. I wanted the entire trip to be a pleasurable experience, and not only in the bedroom department. She and her family hadn't had the easiest of times, and I wanted to treat her. I'd also arranged for her mom to visit one of the best spas in Manhattan. I planned to tell Sage once we were in the air and then have her call her mom and surprise her with it. I'd originally toyed with the idea of just having Filan show up to take her, but I'd decided that carried too much risk. Who knew what she'd spend her free time on after taking care of a disabled child for so long. Sitting indoors might be the last thing she felt like doing.

Filan drew up outside Sage's building, and I climbed out of the back of the car. Smoothing a hand over my shirt, I headed up the path, nerves chewing at my insides, mainly down to apprehension over meeting Lily. I had no experience in dealing with a woman with her particular challenges. She could take one look at me and scream the place down. I'd suggested to Sage a couple times since dinner Friday night that I stop by ahead of today, but she'd dismissed the idea, assuring me Lily would be fine as long as she, Sage, was there.

I'd have to be on my best behavior. No sexual innuendos or double entendres. I'd assume most of those would go over Lily's head if, as Sage explained, she was basically still eight-years-old as far as her mental development went. Despite that, it felt icky. I was a grown man. I could keep my dirty mouth and grabby hands to myself until we'd gotten Lily settled and then headed back to the hotel.

After that, I made no promises.

I raised a hand to knock at Sage's door. It opened before my knuckles made contact against the worn wood. On the other side stood Sage, and tucked into her side, a woman a few inches shorter but with Sage's golden, wavy hair, albeit a few shades lighter, and the same dove-grey eyes. Except whereas Sage's were wise, brought about by her years of experience in the police force, Lily's held an innocence that tugged at my heartstrings. She was a total stunner, yet her mind kept her prisoner. She'd never marry, never have kids of her own. And out of nowhere, a rage swelled within me, similar to the powerful feelings I had for Athena's kidnapper. Some *bastard* had done this to an innocent child, and while her life lay in ruins, he'd walked away without a fucking care in the world.

"Elliot, are you okay?"

Sage's voice pulled me back to the present. I forced down the anger that threatened, knowing the slightest display in front of Lily was not appropriate. She might look like an adult, but she was just a little girl who, I imagined, would scare easily.

I hit her with what I hoped was a reassuring smile. "You must be Lily." I stuck out my hand. "I'm Elliot."

She stared at my hand for the briefest of moments, and then she let go of Sage, flung her arms around my waist and tucked her head underneath my chin. "You brought me the teddy bear."

"I did. Do you like him?"

"I love him." She leaned back and pouted. "I wanted to bring him, but Sage said there wasn't room."

My lips twitched at the petulant display. "You can bring him if you want. There's plenty of room."

"Yesss."

She stuck her tongue out at Sage, and this time, I couldn't suppress my laughter.

"I *told you* it'd be okay, Sage." She disappeared, presumably to fetch the stuffed toy.

"Elliot, there's no way they'll allow us on board with something that size."

I leaned in and brushed my lips over hers, more than pleased when she allowed me to. "Relax. It's fine. I'll take care of it."

"Are you sure? I thought space on planes came at a premium."

"You guys ready to go?" I asked, ignoring her comment. "The car's waiting outside."

"Almost." Sage stood back. "Come on in. I'll be two minutes."

I stepped inside while Sage disappeared into what I presumed was her bedroom. A picture displayed on the mantel caught my eye, and I wandered over to inspect it. I hadn't noticed it the other night. I recognized Sage immediately. I'd say it was taken around the age of sixteen or seventeen. Standing beside her was, I guessed, Lily. A much younger version of the woman she'd grown into. Both girls were smiling into the camera, Sage's braces on full display. I remembered how she used to try to hide those in school, probably to avoid the mean comments that might ensue. Whoever took this photograph had gotten her to smile, though. I wondered who it was.

"Oh God, don't look at that." Sage dashed over and turned it to face the wall. "It's a dreadful picture."

"It's a lovely picture." I picked it up again. "You never smiled like that in high school."

"Can you blame me? With a mouth full of metal and that awful greasy hair. Ugh."

"Your hair wasn't greasy. And loads of kids had braces."

"You didn't."

"Some of us are born gorgeous." I winked.

Sage snorted and rolled her eyes. "Lily, come on. We're going to be late."

Mrs. Abbott appeared, towing a suitcase, with Lily bringing up the rear, the enormous bear I'd brought swamping her. He was rather on the large side, but from the smile on Lily's face, she didn't care.

"Elliot, how lovely to see you again."

"You, too, Mrs. Abbott."

"Call me Jane, please. You're almost family."

Sage growled. "Mother, stop. Just stop."

"I'll take good care of them, Jane." I picked up Lily's suitcase and Sage's overnight bag—although I'd booked the hotel for three nights without telling her. I'd buy her new clothes if she needed them.

"You have a wonderful time, my baby." She hugged Lily tightly, then did the same to Sage. "Call me when you get there."

"We will," Sage replied with a soft kiss on her mother's cheek. "Okay, Mr. Egotistical. Lead the way."

Jane shot her daughter a confused frown, having missed the earlier exchange. Sage didn't explain, just bustled Lily through the door with me trailing behind, a bag in each hand. I'd half expected her to pull the independent woman piece on me and insist she could manage without my help— a fact I didn't dispute. This woman continued to surprise me, often acting differently to how I expected.

Filan waited by the trunk to take our luggage. He'd left both rear doors open. Lily went "Ooh" and dived inside while Sage turned her attention to me.

"A limousine?"

I handed him the bags, then pulled her in for a quick kiss. "The mini vacay starts here, angel."

Her gaze traveled over my face, although I had no idea what she was searching for.

"Thank you. For loaning me the money. For allowing me to do this for Lily and for Mom. For coming with me, even if my mother pushed you into it."

I captured her hand and knitted our fingers together. "First, the money is a gift, not a loan. Don't even try to argue. You won't win. And second, your mother never pushed me into anything. She presented me with an opportunity, and I'm definitely an opportunist. A chance to spend time with you, alone in a hotel where you can't escape me?" I shuddered. "Can't wait."

My eyes challenged her to argue on either point. So it stunned me when she raised herself onto tiptoes and whispered in my ear, "I don't want to escape."

Chapter Fifteen
SAGE

THERE. I'D DONE IT. I'D FINALLY GIVEN IN. I wanted Elliot. He wanted me. We were two grown adults, and not every sexual encounter had to be *going somewhere.* Cass managed casual just fine. In fact, she preferred the excitement of those first few weeks of a new relationship when neither party could keep their hands off each other. Not that I could hand on heart say that'd ever happened to me. If I thought about the two serious-ish relationships I'd had—one lasted six months, the other four—neither had overwhelmed me on the passion front. I hadn't wanted to rip their clothes off or spent most of my day dreaming about seeing them again. I hadn't woken up at night after having the filthiest dream, or masturbated to the image of them— physical or otherwise.

Cass had done all those things several times over. When I shared with her one night that her experiences were alien to me, she'd stared at me, openmouthed, for a good long minute, and then hugged me almost to death and told me how sorry she was. I'd laughed and told her that life wasn't all about sex. She'd vehemently disagreed.

With Elliot, I felt different. He provoked feelings in me I'd never had before. Sometimes I wanted to slap him, other times kiss him, but I couldn't deny the passion between us, and we'd barely touched. An ache grew between my legs. Already I couldn't wait for tonight.

I left him standing there with a shocked expression—damn, it felt good to best him—and climbed into the car. Lily clapped her hands, her excitement off the charts.

"Are we really going on a plane, Sage?"

"We are, Lily Billy." I clipped her seat belt in place as Elliot joined us.

"Don't forget to strap Tubby in," Lily said. "We have to keep him safe, too."

I raked my gaze over Elliot. "He's not that fat."

My joke went right over Lily's head, but not Elliot's. He actually glanced down at himself, then ran a hand over his flat stomach.

I laughed. "Made you check."

His eyes narrowed. "I'll log that transgression away for later."

A quiver inched up my spine, but I hid my delight from him. He didn't need any further encouragement. I appeased Lily by strapping the bear next to her, then I took the seat opposite. Elliot sat beside me, and the car pulled away. Lily's constant chatter and multitude of questions kept us busy, and as the car drew to a halt and Elliot's driver announced we'd arrived, I thought nothing of it as I leaned over, unclipped Lily's and Tubby's belts, and then opened the door and climbed onto the tarmac.

My jaw hit the floor. Okay, not literally, but holy hell. I'd expected to find us at JFK departures surrounded by hundreds of traveling passengers all hurrying to check in. Instead, the only people here were the three of us, Elliot's driver, and a smartly dressed woman in a fitted purple dress with a scarf tied around her neck—who was standing at the top of a flight of stairs leading to a private jet.

"Hey, Fleur." Elliot's voice came from over my left shoulder. "We all set?"

"Absolutely," the woman who I now knew as Fleur, responded. "You must be Sage and Lily. Come on up. We're all ready for you."

Elliot nudged me in the back which unglued my feet from the ground. I took Lily's hand, and she held on to Tubby as we walked up the steps to the plane. I'd only flown once in my entire life. The trip down to Florida when Dad was still alive. There was no comparison between that plane and this one, apart from the fact they both had wings and engines.

Lily followed her "Ooh" at the limo with a "Wow. Neat!" when she disappeared inside. I waited for Elliot to catch up.

"This is yours?"

He nodded. "Better than flying commercial. Make yourself comfortable. I'm just going to have a quick word with the captain. Fleur will get you anything you want."

I watched him walk over to a door, tap on it, and then enter. Overwhelmed, I flopped into a gray leather chair opposite Lily, but her excited grin and pink cheeks soon had me smiling.

"Can I get you a drink?" Fleur asked.

"Just water for me, please. What about you, Lil?"

"Coke."

"Coke, what?"

She coyly glanced up at Fleur. "A Coke, please."

"That's better."

Fleur didn't bat an eyelid at Lily, and I guessed someone had briefed her. Either that or her supreme professionalism meant she kept her thoughts to herself.

"Be right back," she said, then disappeared behind a white gloss screen at the back of the plane.

Lily plunked Tubby on her lap and struck up a conversation with him which gave me a few moments to take in the surroundings. There were four identical chairs in two pairs, each with an oak table between them, a four-seater sofa on the other side of the fuselage, thick wall-to-wall carpeting, and a flat-screen TV that was currently switched off. Knowing the trappings of Elliot's wealth and seeing them, I discovered, were two completely different things. Yeah, I'd seen his house and his cars, but a plane. *A goddamn plane.* Unbelievable.

"Settling in okay?"

I looked up to find Elliot standing beside me. "Yeah. This is... fabulous."

"We'll be taking off soon, so buckle up. Then once we're in the air, I thought Lily might like to visit the cockpit and chat with the captain for a bit."

Lily's eyes went as round as saucers, her conversation with Tubby long forgotten. "For reals?"

Elliot laughed. "Absolutely for reals."

My heart expanded just that little bit more. And that was a dangerous thing.

———

The car that Elliot had arranged to pick us up from the airport wound its way up the impressive driveway, sweeping past manicured lawns, trees in full bloom, and colorful spring flowers dotted along regimented borders. My first thought was that they'd undersold the place in their glossy brochure.

"Sage, look. Horses!" Lily tugged on my arm and pointed at the paddock where several horses grazed, their tails swishing to disperse annoying flies. "Ohhh, they're so pretty."

I caught Elliot's gaze and the momentary sadness in the depths of his eyes as he looked at Lily. I didn't have to be a mind reader to know what he was thinking. What a terrible tragedy. And it was. When she'd been little, her childish mannerisms had fit in with her physical appearance, but as she grew, so did the stares from strangers along with the mumbled explanations, mainly from Mom. Me, I ignored those kinds of ignorant jerks. Most of them thought their rude questions were completely acceptable, and if I allowed myself to react, I'd probably slap the lot of them. Over the years, I'd learned to suppress the anger and the rage at the unfairness of it all. Lily had grown into a beautiful woman, yet she'd never get to do the kinds of things a woman of her age should be enjoying. Work, boyfriends, getting drunk on a Friday night, and spending hours with your head stuck in the toilet.

"They are, sweetheart. I bet you can't wait to pet them."

"I can't." She beamed. "And ride them. I'm so excited."

I gave her a hug as the car stopped in front of an impressive entrance with white pillars framing a cherry-red painted door. The driver opened our door, and by the time we got out, a jolly-looking woman in her mid-thirties dressed in jeans and a flannel shirt was there to greet us.

"You must be Lily."

Ignoring Elliot and me, she dashed over and gave Lily a hug. I immediately relaxed. I loved that she'd put greeting Lily first over me and Elliot. This was the right place, a *good* place.

"Welcome to Foxhill. We are so excited to have you staying here with us for a little while."

"Can I pet the horses?"

"Absolutely. Let's get you settled in first, though. How does that sound? Would you like to see your room?"

Lily beamed. "Yes, please."

The woman turned to us. "I'm Diana. We spoke on the phone." She thrust out her hand, and we shook. "Why don't we all go inside."

We entered the grand building which looked more like a fancy hotel rather than a retreat for people with special needs. Diana beckoned to a young girl around Lily's age.

"This is Maya. She'll be Lily's primary caregiver during her stay with us. Maya, why don't you show Lily to her room and I'll have a quick word with Miss Abbott."

My eyes tracked Lily willingly skipping alongside Maya. I'd expected some reluctance maybe, but no. Lily's incessant chatter faded as she and Maya set off up a set of wide stairs. Yet more evidence she was going to have the time of her life.

"We find they settle in much faster without the family. Strange, I know, but I've been doing this a while, and the evidence speaks for itself."

"Really?"

"Yes." She patted my arm almost like my mom would, even though Diana was closer to my age than my mother's.

"She'll be fine. You must be tired after your long journey. Go get some rest and come back in the morning."

"Are you sure?" I nibbled my bottom lip and glanced at Elliot to get a measure of what he thought about leaving Lily so soon. He gave nothing away. Guess I was on my own with this decision. "Will you call if she's distressed in any way?"

"Yes. Of course."

Elliot's warm palm settled on my lower back, and he applied the gentlest of pressure, a nudge that we should do as Diana suggested.

"Okay," I said reluctantly.

"I'll grab Lily's suitcase," Elliot said, interjecting for the first time since we'd arrived.

He returned less than thirty seconds later, towing her bag behind him. With a final note of reassurance from Diana on Lily's welfare, I left with Elliot. Try as I might, I couldn't rip my gaze away from the building as the car swept down the driveway.

"Relax."

Elliot rhythmically caressed the knuckles on the back of my hand. Back and forth. Back and forth. I let my head sink against the luxurious leather seat and closed my eyes.

"That feels good."

"Just the beginning, angel."

My stomach turned over, and the pulse in my wrist jerked. Elliot lifted my hand. My eyes flew open when his mouth closed around my finger.

"Oh God. I'm in trouble, aren't I?"

A flush of heat built between my legs at his wicked grin.

"The best kind of trouble."

Chapter Sixteen

SAGE

A MAN DRESSED IN A SMART RED UNIFORM WITH gold buttons opened the door almost before the car had come to a complete stop. He stood back, allowing us to step onto a carpet that matched his outfit. I mused whether that was on purpose or by chance. Given the whiff of lavishness I'd gotten in the five seconds that had passed since we'd arrived, I'd say the designers had planned it that way.

"Welcome, Mr. Bancroft."

I shot a glance at Elliot. *A personal greeting?* Did he come here often? Seemed odd.

Elliot gave the man a curt nod. "Thanks."

I peered up at the ornately arched entrance. Elliot's warm palm settled at the base of my spine, and a tremor traveled all the way up to the back of my neck, scattering goose bumps there. From one simple touch. Through clothes. In a non-sexual area.

We stepped into a set of revolving doors. I hated these things, always panicking that I wouldn't move fast enough and the pane of glass behind would smack me in the ass. Fortunately, I emerged unscathed.

"Wow." Slack-jawed, I gaped around the large lobby that screamed opulence. "This is gorgeous."

"Why, thank you." Elliot took my hand. "It's mine."

My already slack jaw almost unhinged from the rest of me. "Yours? You own this hotel?"

"Strictly speaking, it belongs to ROGUES. But as I own a sixth of the company then, yeah, I think that qualifies." He led me over to the reception area where a woman, dressed in a smart gray uniform with gold lettering that read 'ROGUES Hotels' above the pocket, smiled warmly.

"Mr. Bancroft. Welcome to ROGUES Scottsdale. Here are your key cards. The penthouse is all ready for you. I'll have your luggage sent right up."

Penthouse? Oh my God.

Elliot drew the two plastic cards toward himself and slipped them into his pocket. "Great."

With my hand firmly locked inside his again, we crossed the lobby to a bank of elevators. Once inside, Elliot inserted a card into a slot above the number pad, then pressed the PH button. The doors closed with a quiet swish.

"The penthouse?"

His crooked smile did funny things to my insides.

"Wouldn't stay anywhere else. I think you'll like it." He leaned in until his lips touched my ear. "Our first time should be special, don't you think?"

Desire rolled through me, forcing my eyes closed. A soft moan fell from my lips. Elliot gripped my left hip and turned me to face him. He slid his hands up my sides, brushing the outer edge of my boobs.

"You do something to me, Sage. I don't know why

you're different, but you are." He pushed his fingers into my hair, and his mouth covered mine.

Cool air feathered across my neck as the doors whooshed open, but even then, Elliot didn't stop kissing me. Leaning his body into mine, he walked backward, taking me with him. Kissing while walking wasn't as easy as it sounded, and I broke away, giggling. And then the penthouse opened up before me, and I suffered a second metaphorical dislocated jaw. I'd only ever stayed in a hotel twice in my life. Once on the trip to Florida with Mom, Dad, and Lily. I remembered it had been functional and clean, but hardly luxurious. The second time was during a police conference on tackling drug crime that'd taken place down in Washington D.C. That hadn't been great, either. But this... this was on another level completely.

I'd barely taken in the cream leather corner sofa and array of glass vases playing host to colorful bouquets of flowers or the mountain view out the floor-to-ceiling picture windows when Elliot swept me up into his arms. The unexpectedness of it meant I squealed loudly. Unconcerned with a potential burst eardrum, he strode right across the vast space and through another door to a bedroom that was larger than our entire apartment back home. A vast California King bed sat proudly in the center, and at the foot of the bed was a two-seater couch. Another seating area sat off to the left, underneath the window that also looked out onto the red-orange mountain range.

Elliot set me back on my feet and picked up my hands that were hanging loosely by my sides.

"As much as my dick thinks we should fuck fast and hard, I'm thinking we should take it slow. I want to savor every second, rather than have it pass by in a blur. What do you think?"

I blinked a few times. "I think you're a complicated man with layers that continually surprise me. I wouldn't have put you down as an old romantic."

"Less of the old." He gently caressed my cheek with the back of his hand. "You are stunning, and kind, and thoughtful. You make me want to be a better man."

Oh.

He deftly unfastened the buttons on my shirt and slid it down my arms. His gaze locked on my cleavage—yes, I'd invested in a brand-new push-up bra with the knowledge we'd probably end up here—and his tongue swept over his bottom lip. I clenched my thighs. Damn if that wasn't sexy.

He moved on to my jeans, and they joined my shirt on the floor beside the bed. I stood there, in only my bra and panties, while Elliot stared at me as if I was the first woman he'd ever seen almost naked.

"I dreamed of you, of this, of being able to look at you and touch you, but those dreams didn't do you justice."

More of the romantic stuff. I would never have thought it of Elliot. I almost reacted to his compliment with something flippant, but his earnest expression and hungry eyes made me swallow the words. In school he'd been the joker with a quick smile. From the time we reconnected, he'd oscillated between light-hearted sexual innuendos and a dark desire for vengeance that threatened to take down anyone who got in his way. But romance? It just showed how multifaceted he was. Then again, weren't most people?

"Undress me."

His husky voice sent a rush of wetness straight to my core. His chest rose and fell with increasing speed as I slipped my fingers inside his shirt and unfastened the first button. I worked efficiently without rushing. Who needed oysters? Going slow was its own aphrodisiac.

His clothes joined mine. We both stood there, toe to toe, in our underwear, our eyes flicking over each other's bodies. My heart beat so fast, it almost rattled my ribcage, and my mouth watered as if I were about to devour something delicious.

And I was.

Because Elliot worked out. A lot, if the body my eyes were greedily devouring was anything to go by.

I'd suspected as much. In school he'd loved sports. It didn't surprise me that he kept himself fit.

Thank you, God.

"If you keep eying me like that and don't put your hands on me soon," Elliot said with a throaty rasp, "I'll lose my mind."

Dampening my lips, I traced the slight ridge on top of his shoulders, over his protruding collarbone, across his firm chest with a smattering of hairs that tickled my palms. Down I went, outlining each ridge of his abdomen. His muscles rippled beneath my touch, a long shudder rolling through him.

"Two can play at this game, you know," I whispered, sparing him a glance from beneath my eyelashes.

"If I touch you now, I'm going to break my promise to go slow. Hanging on by a thread here, Sage."

"But here's the thing." I brushed the length of his cock through his boxers, and it jerked, begging for me to set it free. "I want you to lose control."

He closed his eyes and breathed through his nose, his nostrils flaring, waging an internal battle with himself. I slipped my hand inside the convenient flap at the front of men's underwear and gripped him, and not gently either, then tugged twice.

He hissed. "Fuck, I'm sorry."

Grabbing my ass, he pulled me into him, and his mouth smashed against mine. Adrenaline and excitement roared through my veins, rendering me panting and breathless. I didn't even feel him unclip my bra, only realizing he had when the tight band around my rib cage loosened. He tore his mouth from mine, sank to his knees, and removed my panties.

"Open your legs, angel."

Oh God.

I shuffled my feet apart, and then his warm mouth was there, at my hot center. He licked me with the flat of his tongue, and I made a sound that in any other moment would send blood rushing to my face, but in this moment with Elliot's dark head between my legs, the only thing that mattered was reaching a climax I'd put off for too long.

I wobbled, and I threaded my hands in his hair to steady myself. "Elliot." His name came out on an expelled breath, that single word filled with want and need and desire.

He circled my clit with his thumb, and the wicked things he was doing with his tongue brought me ever closer to the finish line. Elliot went down on a woman like a man who truly enjoyed it rather than one who only wanted this part out of the way so he could move on to his own pleasure.

My abdomen swelled, a slow build-up of pressure that only had one possible ending. Every single cell in my body screamed *Yes!* Warmth rushed to the apex of my thighs, and my stomach dropped, and then I was coming harder than I ever had in my entire life. I dug my fingers into Elliot's skull, but if it hurt, he didn't complain.

Why did you wait so long?

That was post-orgasm bliss talking. I hadn't been ready to trust Elliot before now, too concerned about being the rebound girl. Damn, though, how glad was I that I'd overcome my worries.

He rose to his feet. With one finger, he swept through my folds then brought it to his mouth, his eyes on me the entire time. My tummy rolled. I couldn't explain why I found that so hot, but it was. He circled my wrist and placed my hand on his erection. If he'd been hard before, now he felt like pure steel.

Elliot groaned as I rubbed him through his boxers. It happened so fast my brain didn't compute the move from the floor to the bed, nor the speed with which Elliot discarded his underwear. My eyes locked on the first unobstructed sight of his cock sticking straight out from between that mouthwatering *V*, a sight rarely seen outside of muscle magazines and the odd celebrity training for a part in the latest action blockbuster.

He leaned over to the nightstand and opened the drawer, removing a still-sealed box of condoms. In seconds he'd torn open the box and a purple foil packet and sheathed his erection. Lining himself up with my entrance, he thrust once, hard, seating himself all the way inside.

It'd been a while for me, and I winced. Elliot paused.

"You okay?" he ground out, his jaw locked up tight as he clung to the last thread of his control.

"God, yes. Move, Elliot."

He didn't need telling twice. He withdrew, almost entirely, then thrust his hips. Our resounding groans got lost in heavy breathing and pleas to fuck me harder. I sensed his approaching orgasm, but as I tightened my inner muscles, he pulled out.

"Turn around. Sit in my lap."

He stroked himself while I maneuvered into position. With my thighs on either side of his, he pushed into me from behind. Hell, that felt full, and good. So, so good. And then the reason for the change of position became apparent. He rolled my nipple between his thumb and forefinger and played with my clit with his other hand, and still managed to thrust into me. Thank God for strong abdominals.

Unbelievably, I felt another orgasm approaching. I didn't need fingers to count the number of times I'd climaxed during the actual sex act. Zero.

"One," I cried out, white spots dancing before my eyes as my insides exploded.

Elliot gripped my hips and controlled the pace and angle, driving into me over and over. He grunted then stilled, his hot breath feathering the back of my neck, his breathing fast and uncontrolled in my ear.

"I'm dead," he muttered.

We collapsed onto the mattress. Elliot removed the condom, then felt for my hand and knitted our fingers together. When we'd recovered, he shifted onto his side and cupped my left breast.

"What does one mean?"

My lips twitched. I was about to feed an ego that was pretty full already, but after that inadvertent shout, there was nowhere to hide. "I've never come during sex. Until now."

A cocky grin edged across his face. "I'm your first?"

I rolled my eyes. "Yes, but let's not make a big deal out of it."

He laughed. "But it *is* a big deal." He tugged me on top of him. "I wonder if I can make you shout *five* before morning?"

Chapter Seventeen

ELLIOT

THE BUTLER WHEELED THE TROLLEY LADEN WITH food over to the dining table. With no clue what Sage liked to eat for breakfast, or even if she skipped it all together, I'd asked the kitchen to send up everything on the menu. He left the plates covered with the stainless-steel warmers, poured two cups of coffee, then retreated. The elevator doors closed as the bedroom door opened.

"Morning." I smiled at Sage and pointed my chin at the table. "Breakfast's here."

She yawned and stretched, and her white camisole top rode up, revealing a sliver of creamy, smooth skin. My dick perked up, although I hadn't a clue how after last night. I was sore, so she must be, too, but if she showed the slightest willingness to go another round, I wouldn't hesitate.

"What time is it?"

"Ten."

"That late?" She scratched her cheek then scanned the room. "Where's my purse? I need to see if Lily's okay."

I gestured to an oak sideboard. "It's over there. She'll be fine. They'd have called if there was a problem."

"I know. I just want to make sure."

She padded across the room, giving me the perfect view of her pert ass encased in satin. I hardened further. *Jesus Christ.* I hadn't gotten this many erections in a twelve-hour period since my college days.

"No calls or messages," she said, relief lightening her soft, grey eyes. "Phew."

"*Now* will you eat?" I removed the tops from the plates. "I didn't know what you'd like."

"So you ordered enough food to feed half of Scottsdale?"

I shrugged. A waste of food, maybe, but the need to cater to Sage's every desire, on this occasion, had trumped doing the right thing.

She sipped her coffee, then helped herself to a pile of scrambled eggs, bacon, and waffles. I smiled to myself. I liked a girl who ate well. Those who nibbled on a lettuce leaf then pronounced themselves full and pushed the rest of their meal around their plates irked me.

Following suit, I piled up my plate, too. Last night's marathon sex session meant my stomach thought I'd put it on rationing.

"Can we go to see Lily right after breakfast?" Sage asked, putting a stop to any ideas of a quickie. "I'd like to spend as much time with her as I can before we leave." She scooped up a forkful of eggs and closed her lips around the tines.

Even harder.

Fuck.

At this rate, I'd have to make an excuse for five minutes alone and take care of this damned erection.

"What time are we flying home?"

"Twelve o'clock."

Sage clasped a hand to her mouth, horrified. "That gives me no time to see Lily. Why didn't you wake me earlier?"

"Twelve o'clock... on Friday." I grinned.

"You... you... asshole."

She threw a croissant at me which I easily caught, and then a laugh erupted from her.

"You almost had me."

"Oh, I definitely had you. Over and over. And now we don't have to rush..." I glanced down at the outline of my erection, clearly visible through my boxers.

"Again? You're voracious."

"Unless you're too sore."

Please say you're not.

"I'm a little sore."

Dammit. Looks as if I'll have to take care of it myself after all, even though that's nowhere near as much fun.

She got to her feet, and then she put the covers over our half-finished breakfast and cocked her head.

"Come on, lover boy. Let's see you do gentle."

I scrambled upright so fast, I almost tripped and head-butted the table. "Yes, ma'am."

―――

My phone vibrated and jumped around on the nightstand. I picked it up and immediately answered.

"Hey, sis. What's up?"

"Where are you? I went to your place this morning and you're not there."

"Correct. I'm in Scottsdale."

"Scottsdale?" I sensed a frown in her tone. "What the

heck are you doing there? You will be back in time for Ethan's baptism, won't you?"

I rolled on my side and played with a strand of Sage's hair.

"Yes, stop panicking. It's not until Sunday."

"With you, Elliot, you never can be sure. I can't have a baptism without the godfather."

"I would have thought the baby was the most important attendee."

"You are such a jerk."

"But you love me."

I nibbled Sage's ear, and she giggled.

"Are you with a woman? Is it Brie?"

I waited for Sage to stiffen at the mention of my ex's name, but she mustn't have heard. Or maybe me playing with her nipple had distracted her.

"No, it's not."

"Oh." A pause, then, "Well, whoever it is, you should bring her with you on Sunday."

Attending an important family event with Sage where all my family and friends would be? Was I ready for that, for the barrage of questions? I'd love to take her as my plus-one, but the ensuing interrogations, from Mom in particular, I could do without.

"Maybe," I said evasively.

"Okay, well just let me know either way." The sound of Ethan's cry reached me. "Gah, he's off again. I gotta go. Bye, Elliot."

I tossed the phone and turned all my attention back to Sage. "Sorry about that. My sister's panicking that I won't be there for my nephew's baptism on Sunday. As if I'd miss that."

"Do you have any pictures of him?"

"Yeah. Wanna see?" I picked up my phone once more and selected the album I'd set up for photographs of Ethan. There were already over five hundred pictures in there. "I love him to death. I always thought babies were boring, but he's awesome."

Sage held my phone and scrolled through. "So cute. How old is he?"

"Almost five months."

She chewed her lip. Every time she did that, I wanted to take over.

"Do you want kids someday?"

I nodded. "Yeah, I do. One day. What about you?"

"Absolutely."

I smiled. "It's good to have this conversation. Make sure we're on the same page. Lots of couples don't, and it causes problems down the line."

Sage laughed. "Stop teasing me. We hardly know each other."

"I disagree. Some people click. For others, it takes forever. Did I tell you that it took Ryker seven years to admit he was in love with my sister?"

Her forehead wrinkled. "Seven years? Wow. That's quite a while. Why did he resist for so long?"

"He worried that I'd lose my shit."

"And did you?"

I sighed heavily. "Yeah. I'm not proud of it."

"You hit him, didn't you?"

"Yep."

Sage gave me a disapproving look. "You really are trouble, Elliot Bancroft."

I took her hand and brought it to my lips. "I might have

a quick temper, and obsess over things more than most, but I'm loyal. I protect the people I care about." I nibbled on the tip of her forefinger. "And I'm kinda cute."

She softly groaned. "I really want to disagree with that, but I can't." She slipped her hand from mine and threw back the covers, then climbed out of bed, skipping out of my reach as I made a grab for her butt. "As cute as you are, my sister comes first. Now move your ass and get dressed."

Chapter Eighteen

SAGE

I MOUNTED THE STEPS TO ELLIOT'S JET AND SANK into the sumptuous leather, resting my head against the back of the chair. My eyes fixed on the seat opposite, the one Lily sat in on our flight down to Arizona.

Returning to New York without her felt strange, but on the three occasions we'd visited her at Foxhill, she'd been having so much fun and had hardly noticed we were even there. I'd miss her terribly, but I left with a light heart in the knowledge that she'd have the time of her life. I'd called Mom several times to update her, and she'd sounded more relaxed than I'd ever heard her. Helped along, no doubt, by the extravagant spa Elliot had arranged for her to visit. I'd castigated him when he'd told me what he'd done, even if his heart had been in the right place. The money meant nothing to Elliot, but enjoying too many luxuries we couldn't afford long term wasn't a great idea. Elliot might have alluded to a more serious relationship during our trip, but I couldn't quite allow myself to believe it.

There were no guarantees, in life or in love. Elliot—or I

—could call it quits tomorrow, and then where would we be?

"Penny for your thoughts?"

Lost inside my mind, I hadn't even seen Elliot sit down. I blinked and offered him a reassuring smile. "Thinking about Lily and what a fantastic time she's going to have." *Not a complete lie.*

"You'll miss her."

A statement, not a question. I answered anyway.

"Enormously. But she needs this. Time away from me. From Mom. And so do we, I guess."

He rubbed the scruff on his chin. "What are you doing Sunday?"

"Nothing in particular." I'd taken the whole week off work, even though I'd assumed we'd only spend a night in Scottsdale, and wasn't due back until Monday. "A long soak in the bath. Maybe read a book."

"Or you could come with me to my nephew's baptism."

I raised my eyebrows and sat up a little straighter. A baptism? Where his parents and his sister would be. Sounded awfully serious suddenly. "Say what now?"

"My nephew's baptism," he repeated, although I'd heard him just fine the first time around. "I promise no one bites." He chuckled. "Apart from me."

"Oh, Elliot. I don't know." I shook my head. "It's a family affair."

"Athena suggested it when I spoke to her on Wednesday after you forced me into having sex... again."

"I did not force—wait. Your sister suggested that you invite me?"

"Yeah. So now will you come?"

I bounced my foot and searched his face for any sign of

doubt. I found none, only an open expression and pleading eyes.

"I'm not sure I have anything suitable to wear." My hand shot in the air as he opened his mouth. I knew what he was about to say, and yeah, that was a resounding no. "Don't. I'll figure it out."

"It doesn't matter what you wear." He flashed a grin. "As long as you wear something, that is. Your naked body is strictly for my eyes only."

I rolled my eyes at him. Elliot was eighty percent light-hearted. It was the unpredictable twenty percent that kept me on edge.

"Everyone is really down-to-earth. They'll make you feel welcome, I promise. It's a small gathering. Twenty or so people. That's it. Ryker and Athena aren't into the whole extravagant bash. Their wedding was a super small event, too."

I grazed my teeth over my lip, still not completely convinced. "Okay, you've got yourself a date."

He looked so pleased that I dared to believe for a brief second we could really have something. And then his next words brought me crashing back to reality.

"Great. Let's make the most of it. Next week, we're back on the trail."

My shoulders dipped. Despite our relationship turning physical, I had to remember that the major reason Elliot wanted me around was to help him on his incessant quest— a hopeless quest in my opinion unless the culprit walked right up to Elliot and confessed. And what kind of idiot would do that after all this time? No doubt they were far too busy enjoying their freedom and the fifty million dollars ransom money.

Elliot filled most of the silence on the flight back to New York. He made no comment on my monosyllabic responses, probably assuming my thoughts were with Lily.

The plane landed fifteen minutes early. Elliot's car and driver waited at the foot of the stairs. An hour later, we pulled up outside my apartment block. Elliot slipped a hand around my neck and drew me in for a kiss.

"I'd love for you to come over to my place for dinner tomorrow, but I guess I should let you have some time with your mom. I'm sure she wants to hear all about Lily."

Despite the altruism behind his comment, his words, following so closely on the heels of his untimely reminder of our deal, stung of rejection. I managed a watery smile.

"Yeah. I'd like to spend some time with her. I'll see you Sunday." I unclipped my belt. "Oh, where am I going and what time?"

Elliot gave me an odd look. "I'll pick you up. Eleven-thirty."

"Oh, sure." Another smile that I knew hadn't reached my eyes. This one he noticed, and a deep frown appeared between his eyebrows.

"Sage, what's wrong?"

"Nothing."

He heaved a sigh. "I have a sister. When she says 'nothing', it usually means 'You'd better duck for cover because I'm going to stab you in the eye with a steak knife.'"

Despite the sadness filling my chest, I snickered. "I'm looking forward to meeting your sister."

He captured my hand and gently caressed my knuckles. "Tell me. I'm a man. We're just not capable of figuring this shit out for ourselves. I don't want to leave things like this. Not after such an idyllic few days."

Left with no option other than to confess, I lifted my chin and looked him squarely in the eye. "What you said on the plane about getting back to the hunt for Athena's kidnapper, it made me feel like that's all you really want from me. You don't want *me,* despite what happened between us in Scottsdale. You just want my investigative abilities."

He couldn't have been more shocked if I'd slapped him in the face. His lips mashed into a grim line, and he shook his head despondently. "That's what you think?" He scrubbed a hand from his forehead down to his chin. "I am such a fuck-wit. And I'm sorry that's how I made you feel. It certainly wasn't intentional. Yes, I want your brilliant mind to help me figure this out, but more than that, the real reason for my eagerness, is that I get to spend more time with you. If we succeed—and I'm confident we will—then great. But that isn't all I want. Not anymore. I admit, in the beginning, that was the principal reason, but if you think back, I also made no secret of the fact I wanted you. And I still want you. Now more than ever."

He undid his seat belt and shuffled closer, gathering me in his arms. He kissed me, stealing every molecule of oxygen from my lungs, leaving me breathless.

"Sunday can't come fast enough," he muttered, our lips still connected. "I'll book a room at the Plaza. There's no way I'll manage to keep my hands off you all day."

The Plaza? Well, that settles it. I'll have to go shopping, and damn the bank balance.

"I'll see you Sunday."

———

The god of good fortune—whoever the hell he or she was— must've been smiling down on me because I found a gorgeous mint-green Donna Karan dress in Macy's at half off. Still way too rich for my meager savings, but I could hardly turn up to a bash at The Plaza, hosted by billionaires no less, in an off-the-rack from Target. Too bad I couldn't afford designer shoes and a purse to match. At least the black heels and simple clutch didn't look too out of place. With any luck, they'd have dim lighting, and I'd get away with it.

Elliot texted to let me know the Brooklyn Bridge was backed up, meaning he'd be a little late. I paced while I waited until Mom huffed and told me to sit down before I wore a hole in a carpet we couldn't afford to replace. Another thirty minutes of bouncing knees, picking at imaginary fluff, and checking my watch, my phone buzzed.

I'm outside. I'd come up, but we're running late. Say hi to your mom for me.

I leaped to my feet and smoothed a hand over my hip. "He's here. Do I look okay?"

"You look beautiful. Now stop worrying. Just because they have money doesn't make them any better than you."

I kissed her cheek. "Wise words, Mom. Elliot says hi by the way, but we're going to be late if we don't leave now."

"Sage, go. Your panicking is giving me a headache."

I chuckled. Mom rarely minced her words. I wrapped a pale-green scarf around my shoulders and picked up my purse.

"Bye."

The one and only elevator still had a huge 'Out of Order' sign stuck to it. Mom told me it'd broken down the day after I'd left for Arizona, and despite promises from the building superintendent that it was a priority, here we were, almost a week later.

I ducked into the stairwell and emerged into a bright and sunny day. The smell of spring was in the air, and after a long winter, I craved the lighter nights and warm weather before the oppressive heat of summer hit. Spring was my favorite season, and I smiled as I made my way to Elliot's limo. He climbed out to greet me, his eyes traveling from my head to my feet and back up again.

"Are you trying to kill me with that dress?" He slipped his arms around my waist and leaned down for a kiss. "Stiffies at baptisms are not appropriate."

"Is sex all you think about?"

"When you're around, pretty much, yeah. When we're not together, I manage to put it out of my mind a few minutes at a time."

"Go you."

He waited for me to get in the car, then walked around the back and climbed in beside me. We got lucky with the traffic on the way into Manhattan, arriving at The Plaza only fifteen minutes late according to Elliot.

"Don't worry. I texted ahead. Besides, I'm the godfather. They can't start without me."

"Hmm. Didn't you tell your sister on the phone that the baby was the most important part of the ceremony?"

He narrowed his eyes. "Your memory is far too good."

I tapped my temple. "You'd better believe it."

Elliot linked our hands, and I took comfort in the warmth of his palm and the strength of his fingers wrapped around mine. My heart climbed with every step. Meeting family was a nerve-racking moment at the best of times, let alone at a baptism. Not to mention Elliot's family and friends would be far more familiar with his ex and would likely jump to the conclusion he was on the rebound, further adding to my own worries on that matter. The ones that just wouldn't quit.

"Your hands are sweating." Elliot gave me a reassuring squeeze. "Relax. They are going to love you."

"I should have worn my cop uniform."

Elliot's lips quirked up at the corners. "Why? Are you planning to arrest someone?"

"No. It's just... I don't know. I'd feel more confident."

Elliot let go of my hand, then stroked my back. "It's only my family and my best friends, Sage. They're good people."

"But what if... oh, never mind."

Elliot stopped, adding further to our tardiness. He seemed unconcerned at keeping his sister waiting even longer. "Finish the sentence, Sage."

I gazed into his amber irises with those flecks of gold around the edges and sucked in the deepest breath. "What if they compare me to your ex?" *There. I said it.*

He released a long sigh. "Angel, there is *nothing* to compare. You have integrity and morals. She had a penchant for personal trainers. And besides, you're far more beautiful."

His words were meant to reassure. Instead, they irritated. "Don't patronize me. I saw her that night, remember. She was stunning."

"There's nothing attractive about a woman who cheats." He ran his hands up my sides. "It's been almost three months since I caught her fucking that guy. Would you like to know how many times she's crossed my mind in that time?"

Biting on my lip, I nodded.

"Every time *you* bring her up. That's it. She doesn't even register. My mind is too full of you. There isn't room for another woman."

My jaw slackened. *Well, fuck me.*

"Now please, can we never mention her again? I'm excited to introduce you to everyone I care about, although I probably should have warned you to expect a severe grilling. Not in a bad way," he rushed on to say, probably noticing my dismayed expression, "just in a 'desire to get to know you' way."

I smiled tentatively. "Okay, let's do it."

"Thank Christ." He eased up the cuff of his shirt and checked his watch. "Because if we're much later, Athena is going to knee me in the balls, and then what use will I be to you?"

Giggling, I walked alongside him. We strode down a carpet so thick my heels sank into the fibers. My gaze fell on a stunning woman with dark wavy hair cascading to her waist, and the same amber eyes as Elliot's, except hers were flashing with annoyance and she tapped her foot repeatedly.

Athena. It had to be Elliot's sister. The family resemblance was astonishing.

"About time," she said. "Then again, you always do like to make an entrance." Her annoyance dissipated as she turned to face me, her arms outstretched in welcome. "You must be Sage. I'm so glad you could come."

She stepped forward, clutched both my upper arms, and kissed me on the cheek. My nerves ebbed away.

"Thank you for inviting me. It's lovely to meet you."

"We'll have a proper chat later. But if we don't start the baptism soon, I'm worried the minister will need a heart surgeon."

Elliot whispered, "Told you," then held my hand and followed Athena inside.

The introductions passed in a blur, but the welcome couldn't have been any warmer. By the time we'd sat down, I'd already forgotten most of the names. Elliot left me with one of his friends—who, luckily for me, reintroduced himself as Sebastian—and went to stand at the front with Athena and Ryker. I'd identified him immediately. He'd matured, like we all had, but I wouldn't have failed to recognize him.

The actual ceremony only took a few minutes. Elliot returned to my side and walked with me to an adjoining room where a beautiful buffet stretched almost the length of an entire wall. My stomach rumbled as the delicious smells wafted across the room. I clamped my arm across my middle.

"Hungry?" Elliot asked, his eyes twinkling.

"I missed breakfast," I said by way of explanation. "Too nervous."

"I'm starving, too." He bent his head and touched his lips to my ear. "But not for food."

Heat licked through my veins, and a pleasurable shudder rippled up my back. "Yeah, I need the food."

Elliot threw back his head and laughed. "Come on, let's go and say a proper hello to Athena and then I'll feed you."

Chapter Nineteen

ELLIOT

Thinking about sex at my nephew's baptism ceremony is inappropriate.

But Sage wasn't making it easy. Her green dress hugged every single curve, including her ass, which I'd finally admitted I was more than a little obsessed with. During our trip to Arizona, a switch had flicked inside my head. What had started out as a physical attraction to a woman whose help I needed to help me solve a four-year-old mystery had morphed into a craving to spend every spare minute in her company. Not only to fuck either. I enjoyed talking to her. She made me laugh, and for the first time in years, I didn't spend every waking moment plotting what I'd do when I finally caught up with the man who'd taken my sister.

Make no mistake, despite Sage's robust warnings about cold cases, that bastard wouldn't get away with it. But when I was with her, she crowded out the venomous thoughts and helped me return to the man I used to be. More joyous, less angry.

"You've changed," Ryker said to Sage as we approached him and Athena. "But not really, if that makes sense."

She smiled. "It's the lack of braces and pimples."

"I couldn't believe it when Elliot told us it was you who'd arrested him." Ryker shot me an evil grin. "Probably should have left him in the slammer for a few more days."

"Fuck off."

"Language," Athena said, shifting Ethan to her other hip. "Babies pick up on things."

I plucked my nephew from my sister's arms and swung him in the air. He giggled and crushed my heart. Damn, I loved this kid.

"You'll forgive your Uncle Elliot for cussing, won't you, Ethan?"

"He might, but *I* won't if the first word out of his mouth is a curse word," Athena said.

My gaze fell on Sage who was gazing at Ethan with a mixture of wonderment and longing. She reached out and wiggled Ethan's foot, drawing another giggle from him.

"Do you want to hold him?" I asked.

Sage checked in with Athena who smiled and nodded her approval.

"You can if you want to. I'm not one of those weird mothers who hovers over anyone holding her precious cargo."

I placed Ethan in Sage's arms. As I watched her cradle him and press a soft kiss to his forehead, a tight band stretched across my chest. Out of the corner of my eye, I saw Ryker watching me. I met his puzzled gaze and shrugged. His eyes widened as he caught on. Brie and I had dated for over four years, and I'd never once felt that urge to have a child with her, yet with the woman standing before me holding my treasured nephew, I could totally imagine it. Not that planned to say that to Sage. It'd taken enough persuasion to get our relationship this far. If I mentioned having kids for a second time, she'd probably run a mile.

I recognized the oddness of this situation. Normally it was the woman trying to coax a man into having kids, and the guy backing off as if she'd threatened to douse him in acid. I believed it was the combination of my sister giving birth, finally ending a relationship after a long-overdue period of avoiding the truth, and meeting Sage. All three had combined into the perfect storm of maturity.

"Elliot, got a minute?"

Ryker cocked his head, signaling for me to follow him.

I glanced at Sage.

"I'm fine. You go."

"She'll be good here with me," Athena added. "We'll gripe and moan about men. Oh, and here comes Mom. She'll join in."

I shot a glance over my shoulder. "Wonderful," I said with as much sarcasm as I could push into a single word. Both women sniggered.

I detoured into Mom's path, warned her not to grill Sage to within an inch of her life, and briskly followed my best friend. Ryker stood with one foot braced against the wall and his arms hanging loosely by his sides.

"If the hotel manager sees you scuffing up his expensive wallpaper, he'll have a coronary," I said.

He shrugged, unconcerned. "He can bill me."

"What's up?"

"How've you been? We've hardly seen you since..."

"You fired me?" I chuckled to let him know there were no hard feelings. We hadn't spoken about it after he'd told me the day following my arrest that I was being cut out of the business, albeit temporarily. It was too painful for either of us to rake over every five minutes, so we'd avoided the subject altogether. "It's not intentional." I refrained from telling him that I'd used the time to pore over ever-diminishing scraps of evidence. At least I had for the first few weeks. Lately, it was Sage taking up all my time.

"You seem different. More like your old self."

"I haven't given up, Ryker," I said, a twinge of pain twisting in my gut as the glimmer of hope in his eyes faded. "And I doubt I ever will. Not completely. But yeah, I think it's safe to say that searching for the truth no longer consumes every second of my life."

"Do we have Sage to thank for that?"

I held his gaze, warmth flooding my chest. "I'm crazy about her."

Ryker cracked a broad smile. "You look happy, Elliot. Christ, I've fucking missed you."

"Don't get all maudlin on me."

He pulled me into a rough hug, clapping me on the back. "I spoke to the rest of the guys. We all want you to come back. It's awful not having you around, even when you are being a complete dick."

My eyebrows shot up, wrinkling my forehead. I hadn't seen that coming. "You're serious?"

"Deadly. But," he raised his finger in the air, silencing me from further comment, "ROGUES must be your priority. We can't have a fuck-up like last time. We're only as good as our last deal."

"That'll never happen again. I'll give it my all. Fuck, I've missed the buzz, and you bunch of jerks."

Ryker grinned and slung an arm around my shoulder. "Let's go get a drink and some food."

The second we stepped into the room, a round of applause greeted us, and I found myself in the middle of a swarm of my best friends. I received so many wallops on the back, I'd definitely have a bruise or two in the morning. Bastards must've known why Ryker had taken me outside.

When they finally released me, I sought out Sage. I found her flanked by Mom and Athena, with Dad hovering off to the side. Her smile lit me up from the inside. Crossing the room, I clasped her hand.

"Borrowing my girl for a minute."

I towed her behind me and out into the hallway. A short distance away, I found a small, private alcove. Backing her into it, I caught her hips and tugged her closer to me.

"What's the matter?" she asked, concern written all over her face. "Athena told me what Ryker was planning to do. Aren't you happy?"

"Ecstatic, but not nearly as happy as I am when I'm with you."

Her eyes softened, and her gaze fell to my lips. She curved her hands around the back of my neck and kissed me. In three seconds, we went from PG to way above NC-17. Any minute now, there'd be a hand on my shoulder and the management would eject us for lewd conduct.

Reluctantly, I drew back, pecking her lips to soften any idea of rejection she might get in that pretty head of hers. "I said something to Ryker before, and I'm pissed at myself because you should have been the first person I told."

Her eyebrows arrowed inward, forming a deep frown. "What?"

I smoothed the creased skin with my thumb, then

pressed my lips there. "I told him I was crazy about you. And I am. So fucking crazy. This isn't casual for me, Sage. It's so much more than that. I'm yours and you're mine. Okay?"

"Oh, Elliot." She held her palm to her chest. "You old romantic."

I chuckled. "Angel, you ain't seen nothing yet."

Almost as though her lips were a magnet to mine, this time, I kissed her.

"Do you think anyone would notice if I whipped you upstairs for a quickie?" I asked. "I booked the room."

On cue, her stomach rumbled. Looked as if fate had stepped in and forced me to wait to get her into bed.

"Can we at least eat? I'm starved."

"Okay, but eat fast." I hesitated. "But not so fast you get sick."

We headed back toward the function room, giggling like a pair of teenagers, almost as we should have been back in high school if we'd plucked up the courage to be honest about our feelings. As we approached the entrance, a woman somewhere around her early forties appeared to my left.

"Elliot? Elliot Bancroft?"

I frowned. She wasn't familiar to me. "Yes. Who wants to know?"

"My name is Helen Carruthers. You don't know me." She dabbed at her forehead with a tissue. "I'm married to your father."

I snort-laughed. "My mother is married to my father."

"I'm talking about your real father."

Ice shot through my veins. My body language must have given me away because Sage stepped closer. But even her warmth couldn't chase away the chill in my bones.

"He *is* my real father. If you're talking about that piece of shit sperm donor, then I'm sorry for you."

I went to brush by her. She put out her arm.

"Please. You and your sister are the only people who can help me."

I loomed over her. I didn't need to see my face to know what she'd see. Fury, vengeance, hatred.

"Is he here?"

If he'd shown up to Ethan's baptism, I'd rip out his heart and ram it down his throat.

"No. No, he doesn't even know I am. Hear me out. It's all I ask."

"No." I flattened my hand to Sage's lower back and urged her forward. Adrenaline prickled my skin, and my heart raced, and not in a good way. That *bastard*. I'd sent him packing years ago. And now some poor bitch he'd married had the gall to seek me out on my nephew's special day to ask for help. Anything to do with *him* was poison. And that included her. She'd get nothing from me. *Nothing*.

"My son is sick," she called out. "We've tried everything. You're my last hope."

So that's what she wanted. Money. I might've known. I didn't believe for a second that he had no clue she'd come here today. He was behind this. It was always about the mighty dollar for him. He probably thought sending a woman and trying to use a kid to his own advantage might work in his favor.

I spun around slowly. "You have a kid? With him?"

She nodded. "Your half brother." She rummaged in her pocket, producing a picture. "His name's Thomas. He's ten."

I refused to look at it. "I can't help you. And if you come

anywhere near my sister or my family, I promise you will regret it. Leave and don't come back. And tell that lowlife to crawl back to the fucking sewer where he belongs."

Without sparing her another glance, and with Sage jogging to keep up with me, I strode off. Meeting her had ruined the day, and a sixth sense I couldn't explain told me that wasn't the last of it.

This time, when I sent my bastard sperm donor packing, it'd be for good.

Chapter Twenty

SAGE

ELLIOT FIRMLY GRIPPED MY ELBOW AND STEERED me back into the function room. "Not a word to Athena, Ryker, or my parents," he warned. "I don't want any of them to hear of this."

"What if she comes back?" I asked.

"I'll deal with it." His jaw flexed, and his free hand clenched into a tight fist, whitening his knuckles.

Despite my earlier hunger, I struggled to swallow much of the delicious array of food. Elliot tried to keep up a pretense that all was well, but the earlier amiable smile and twinkling eyes had vanished. He managed to convince most people that nothing was wrong, but at one point, Ryker caught my eye and raised a brow in question. I simply shrugged and grinned, hoping to convey to him not to worry.

I'd never seen the kind of hatred that Elliot had shown for his father, not even on the only other occasion he'd mentioned him, the night we'd first gone out for dinner. I hoped, for both their sakes, that his wife had been telling the truth and she really had come without his knowledge. I dreaded the fallout if Elliot came face to face with his dad.

As the time passed, Elliot grew more and more sullen, drawing into himself. I tried to keep his spirits up, but his responses faded to almost nothing apart from the odd curt yes or no. Concerned that his family might ask him a direct question along the lines of "What the hell is wrong with you?", I waited for a moment alone to present itself, then I leaned in and quietly whispered, "Do you want to leave?"

"Don't be fucking ridiculous," he snapped. "I can't exactly walk out of my nephew's baptism."

I pulled in my lips and breathed deeply through my nose. "Yet you were willing to earlier for the sake of a quick screw." I'd had enough. "Fine, Elliot. You stay, but I won't be spoken to like that. I'm not your whipping post. I'm leaving."

I scanned the room, spotting Athena and Ryker standing with... maybe Garen? I hadn't gotten the names of everyone locked in yet. I left Elliot simmering in his anger and crossed the room to say my goodbyes and thank them for inviting me. Halfway there, Elliot's hand landed on my shoulder.

"Sage, wait. I'm sorry."

Keeping my voice low—I didn't want to draw attention to our disagreement—I stared into his bleak eyes and shook my head. "I think we should call it quits for today, Elliot, before one of us says something we might regret. I know you're angry. Hell, it's coming off you in waves, but that isn't *my* fault, nor Athena's nor Ryker's or anyone else here. If you want to avoid questions you'd rather not answer, then I suggest you up your acting skills because eighty percent of this room have already noticed something's wrong."

I slipped out of his grasp and continued over to Athena. "Sorry to interrupt," I said, pasting on a fake smile. "I'm afraid I have to leave. Family stuff. But thank you so much for inviting me. I had a lovely time." I peered into the bassinet where Athena had put her baby down for a brief nap. "He really is gorgeous."

Athena shot a look over my shoulder at, I guessed, Elliot. Whatever she saw made her brow wrinkle. Her eyes returned to mine. "We were so glad you could come." She hugged me. "I don't know what's going on," she whispered in my ear, "but try not to be too hard on him. He can be an asshole, but his heart is in the right place."

Her words brought a genuine smile to my face. "Thank you. I hope we meet again sometime."

"There isn't a doubt in my mind."

I turned away, brushed straight past a stricken-looking Elliot, and headed for the exit. Half of me wanted him to chase after me, and the other half fretted that I might slap some sense into him if he did.

"Sage, wait."

I continued walking, upping my pace until the lobby came into view. I'd stop eventually, but we weren't having this discussion with his friends and family as an involuntary audience.

"Please."

At the pleading tone in his voice, I drew to a halt but didn't turn around. Slowly, he appeared in my line of sight. He shot me an apologetic smile.

"I didn't mean to snap. It's all come as a bit of a shock."

I let the silence linger in the air.

"You're right. Speaking to you like that is unforgiveable. I... just... please don't leave. Not like this. I... I need you."

I released a long sigh. "Elliot, I know you have a lot of deep-seated issues with your birth father, but that isn't my fault, nor that woman's, and definitely not her son's. Aren't you curious what she wanted?"

"I know what she wanted," he bit out, bitterness changing the cadence of his voice. "Money. And the whole bullshit excuse that he didn't know she'd come." He barked a sarcastic laugh. "Of course he did. He sent her."

"But why now? After all these years? You told me your father came to you asking for money after he served his time in prison. But that was a long time ago. Where has he been? And why hasn't he asked you for money until today?"

He repeatedly flexed his fingers. "I don't know and I don't care, but anyone connected with that man is poison, including his wife and their son. I don't want that woman-beating bastard anywhere near me or anyone I care about, and that includes you."

I couldn't quite think of an innocent child as poison, but right this second, there was no reasoning with Elliot. He needed to cool down, and once he had, then I might be able to have a civilized conversation with him. The police officer in me was curious to know more. My mind kept coming back to where she'd said her son was sick. It took a special kind of evil to use your child to extort money, and something in her expression told me she wasn't lying. Call it women's intuition.

Elliot brushed a hand over my hair, then fed a lock of it through his fingers. "Am I forgiven?"

My heart softened toward him. "I suppose so. But speak to me like that again, and I'll see to it that you never father children. Are we clear?"

He broke out into a broad grin. "Crystal. But you might

want to rethink stripping me of my ability to procreate. If I can't have kids, then neither can you, and given what a great mom I think you'll make, that would be a crying shame."

My stomach flipped as I caught on to his meaning. He really was serious about me, about us, about the future. This was moving fast, but instead of pulling back, I wanted to jump in with both feet and see where the wild ride took me. Life with Elliot would never be boring. Infuriating at times. But always exciting.

"I'll consider it," I said. "Besides, I have lots of other equally painful punishments in my toolbox."

He fake shuddered. "You say the sexiest things. How about we go make use of that room upstairs and you can show me your tools?"

I chuckled, shaking my head at the same time. This man was incorrigible, and I couldn't resist him.

"Shouldn't you return to Ethan's baptism? You were very insistent earlier?"

A touch of crimson darkened his cheeks. Damn, he was cute when he blushed.

"Athena will approve of my early exit if it means you and I have made up. Besides, it's almost over anyway." He pressed his hands together in prayer. "Come on, Sage. Take pity on me." His voice lowered. "My dick misses you. He hasn't seen you since Friday morning."

I bit back a giggle. "Are you talking about your penis as if it's a person?"

"Trust me, he has a mind," Elliot muttered. "A one-track mind."

Laughter burst from my chest, loud enough that a couple of passersby cast me odd looks. I'd almost forgotten we were standing just off the lobby in The Plaza.

"Maybe we should take this conversation elsewhere."

"Like upstairs?" Elliot's face lit up with hope.

"I don't think conversation is what you have in mind if we go upstairs?"

"Sure it is," Elliot said. "I can fuck and talk at the same time."

An elderly lady, at least eighty-years-old, who happened to pass at the wrong time, gasped. Elliot saluted her. I grabbed his arm and towed him toward the elevators before the hotel tossed us out. As the doors closed behind us, he flashed an impish grin.

"I knew I'd win."

He crowded me, encasing me with his warm, solid body. His lips closed over mine, firm but coaxing. His tongue gently stroked and tangled with my own. And all the angst and arguments, the hurt and anger, they all melted away, leaving only me and Elliot, this man I shouldn't fall for.

Too late. I already have.

The ding of the elevator broke the spell, and we separated. Elliot locked our hands together, and we turned left out of the elevator, walking a short way down the hallway. He fished a keycard from his trouser pocket and tapped it against the door. A sound bleeped, and the lock sprang open. Elliot gestured for me to enter ahead of him.

"It's not the penthouse suite, but it's got a great view of the park."

He kicked the door closed with his heel and snagged me around the waist. I expected him to kiss me, but he gazed into my eyes instead.

"I am going to make it up to you for my awful behavior today."

"It wasn't all bad." I blinked up at him. "I liked the part

where you said you were crazy about me, and the kissing bits were good, too."

"Is that so?" He proved his point by kissing me again until I ran out of air and came up gasping.

Elliot inched down my zipper, and my expensive, bought-on-credit Donna Karan dress dropped to the floor. I tried not to wince at the idea of it getting creased or, worse, trodden on. But then Elliot crouched, picked it up, and gently laid it over a nearby chair. He returned to me, his heated gaze almost flaying my skin.

"Every time I look at you, I feel it. Right here." He pressed a clenched fist to his chest. "I can't imagine a life without you in it."

Oh my.... Wow.

I tried to find the right response, but each one sounded trite and not at all what Elliot deserved. Most men hardly ever put themselves on the line like that, yet Elliot wasn't afraid of showing his emotional side. And God, it worked. I'd never found him more attractive than right this second.

I traced his jawline, feeling the scruff beneath my fingers. "I'm going nowhere."

He groaned, a low rumble that reverberated through his chest. Encircling my waist, he lowered his head and kissed the spot where my neck met my shoulder. A shudder rolled down my spine. I threw back my head, giving him more room to devour me, and buried my hands in his soft hair. I pulled gently on the roots.

"I love it when you kiss my neck."

I felt his smile. He continued dropping tender kisses along my collarbone, adding in the odd flick of his tongue. He walked me backward. My knees hit the frame of the bed. I fell onto the mattress, and Elliot followed.

"Someone's in a hurry." He bit down on my earlobe. "I approve."

"Then you'd better get your clothes off."

He kneeled up, shrugged out of his jacket, unfastened his tie, ripped three buttons while removing his shirt, and managed to take off his trousers without standing.

"Impressive." I giggled.

He rolled to the side, taking me with him. "You, on top. I like the view." Reaching up, he unclipped my bra, and his hands covered my breasts. "Damn, I love your tits."

I slipped the tip of my finger along the waistband of his boxers, then dipped inside that handy little pocket at the front and took out his cock. I circled the tip with my thumb, spreading the moisture all over the head. Elliot flopped back against the pillows and sighed deeply.

"I hear you've missed me." I bent forward and kissed the tip.

He hissed through his teeth. "He's missed you a lot. A whole lot."

I smiled, tightened my grip, tugged twice, and then pulled him inside my mouth.

He arched his back and raised his arms overhead, gripping the headboard. "Fuck. Jesus. Yes. Just like that."

My core clenched. Damn, why did I find sucking Elliot off such a turn-on? When we were in Scottsdale, I'd taken the opportunity whenever it presented itself. I adored the little noises he made, and the look of pure bliss that spread across his face as his orgasm hit. I'd made excuse after excuse with my previous boyfriends not to put my mouth anywhere near their dick. Then again, I hadn't been in love with them.

No. That couldn't be right. I wasn't in love with Elliot. We'd only taken our relationship to the next level last week.

Then again, the tension between us had been building for months, and that came on top of the unrequited obsession in high school.

Maybe I was in love with him.

Oh God.

Was this bad or good?

I didn't have the answer.

"Keep going," Elliot encouraged, and only then did I realize I'd frozen mid-suck. Forcing the shocking revelations to the back of my mind, I gave Elliot my full attention. He tensed, mumbled some incoherent words, and then his warm, salty essence flooded the back of my tongue.

His hands tangled in my hair, and I raised my head. He gazed down at me with hooded eyes.

"Come here."

I crawled up his body, and his muscular forearms came around my waist, holding me in place. He kissed me, and it felt like a thank you.

And then I found myself beneath him. He gazed down at me, a tender smile turning up the corners of his mouth.

"I thought you liked the view?"

"Oh, I do. I just need a little recovery time, and I know exactly how I plan to spend it."

He shimmied down my body and slowly drew my panties down my legs. He pressed his hands against my thighs, parting them.

"Damn, you're so wet. My dick might've missed you, but I've missed this."

He pressed a kiss to my clit, then blew on it. My hips jerked.

"Lie back and relax, angel. I have a lot of making up to do."

Chapter Twenty-One

ELLIOT

"What time is it?"

Wearily, I lifted my arm and checked my watch. "Six. Shall I call room service and have dinner sent up?"

"I need to call Mom and let her know I'll be late."

I slipped my hand around Sage's neck and drew her in for a lingering kiss. "Stay the night."

"I can't. I have work tomorrow. All my stuff's at home."

"I'll drive you home early. You can grab your things and then I'll drop you right at the precinct."

A flicker of indecision crossed her face, then she shook her head. "Not tonight."

I crammed down disappointment, my eyes lowering to her bare ass as she crossed the room to fetch her purse. My dick rose to the occasion, surprising even me. It'd seen more action in the last week than it had in months, and yet somehow, it wasn't enough. With Sage, I didn't think it would ever be enough.

Not for the first time, I wondered if our lives would've taken different paths had we fessed up to our mutual crush in high school. Maybe we'd have married and had a couple of kids, or perhaps college and ROGUES would've torn us apart? That mystery would remain unsolved, but given the strength of the feelings coursing through me, I bet we'd have found a way to stick together.

I picked up the house phone and ordered two steak dinners and a bottle of red wine. When I replaced the receiver, Sage had finished talking to her mom. I held out my arms, beckoning her back to bed. She snuggled into my side, and I kissed the top of her head.

"All okay at home?"

"Yeah. You know, I rather think she's enjoying the time to herself. I worried she might feel lonely, but when I spoke to her just now, she told me she's planning a long soak in the bath, a glass of wine, and then turning in for the night with a great book."

"She's had it tough. You both have. She deserves some relaxation. Spending time alone can be good for us."

"We're not the only ones who've had it tough."

Shifting onto her side, she propped herself up on her elbow and traced my abs with her fingertip. They rippled beneath her touch.

"I'm worried about you."

I wrinkled my brow. "Me? Why?"

"When Helen turned up out of the blue earlier today, I've never seen such hatred in a person's face as you had for your father. It scared me."

Her words punched me in the gut. I caressed the back of my hand over her cheek. "There's no need to be scared. I'd never lay a finger on you or any other woman. The idea of violence toward women turns my stomach."

"I'm not scared for me, Elliot. I'm scared for *you*. That

kind of revulsion poisons a person from the inside. It isn't healthy. Don't let your father win. Don't let him steal the person you are. You need to let it go."

I fisted the sheets, anger burning my insides like the furnace on a steam train. I only realized I'd clenched my jaw tight enough to grind out my fillings when it began to ache. Sage flattened her palm on my stomach. I shrugged her off and sat up, clutching the edge of the mattress until my knuckles turned white.

"No."

Launching out of bed, I crouched to pick up my boxers. I pulled them on and stuffed my arms into my shirt.

"Elliot."

I spun around. "This isn't up for discussion, Sage. That man deserves every ounce of my hatred. What he did to my mother was unforgiveable."

"I didn't say forgive him. I said let it go."

"Same damn thing."

Sage climbed out of bed and disappeared into the bathroom, returning swaddled in a hotel robe. She stood in front of me, gently rubbing her palms up and down my arms. God, she was good for me. Somehow she always managed to soothe my rage.

"Letting the hatred go isn't the same as forgiving the person. I've never forgiven the man who caused Lily's injuries, but I had to find a way to come to terms with the consequences. To keep carrying all that anger inside... eventually it'll eat you up. And you're carrying two lots of rage. One for your father and the other for Athena's kidnapper. That's dangerous, Elliot. If you don't at least try to put this behind you, one day, you're going to explode, and I fear for anyone caught in the crossfire."

I hung my head. "I can't. I'm sorry if that disappoints you. You might've moved on, but I just don't know how to."

She eased up my chin until I met her gaze. So much emotion swirled in her soft gray eyes. "You haven't disappointed me, Elliot. You've saddened me."

I winced. She didn't mean her words to sting, but fuck, they did.

Forcing a smile, I twirled a lock of her hair around my forefinger. "Don't be sad. Not on my account. I rarely spare him a thought. What happened today just brought him front and center in my mind. Tomorrow, I'll have forgotten all about it."

"And if Helen comes around again? Will you hear her out? Because I can't help thinking this isn't about money."

I snorted. "Trust me, it is." I breathed out heavily. "Can we change the subject? Our dinner will arrive soon. I just want to enjoy a meal with you before you up and leave me alone. All alone. And sad. So terribly sad."

A hint of a smile curved her lips upward. "Crazy man."

I flashed her a wicked grin. "Admit it. That's the attraction."

———

Sage disappeared inside her building, and a void opened up in my chest. I'd joked about her leaving me sad and alone, but inside, that was exactly how I felt. At least I had work to occupy my time. Given Sage had broken the news that she had five full shifts coming up, which meant I wouldn't see her until next Saturday, I needed the distraction. Ryker and the guys had come through for me right on time. I was lucky he hadn't witnessed my angry exchange with that woman,

Helen. He might've changed his mind about my suitability to return to the office if he had.

But as Filan drove me home, curiosity nibbled at my insides. Somewhere in this world Athena and I had a half brother. One who, if his mother had told the truth, was sick. I bet they needed money for his medical bills. Even if they had insurance, the cost of medical care wasn't cheap, and I doubted my father—God, I despised thinking of him in those terms—my sperm donor had spare cash lying around. Even when he and Mom were together, they'd lived paycheck to paycheck, never quite hauling themselves out of the continual cycle of work, bills, more work, more bills. Things only improved financially after he got sent down, and Mom met Karl, my real dad. Karl ran a successful business in his own right, and while we'd not exactly had money to burn, growing up we'd lived in a nice house, taken a vacation every year, and hadn't wanted for a damn thing.

I didn't have it in me to embrace a half brother. Financial resources, on the other hand. That I could offer help with. By the time I arrived home, I'd made up my mind. If Helen came around again, I'd give her whatever she needed to pay for her son's medical treatment. He was an innocent in all of this. Or maybe I shouldn't wait for her, in case I'd well and truly scared her off. It might be a better idea to do a little digging, find out where they lived, and send a check in the mail.

Sage would approve, and that was more than enough reason to do it.

It was almost eleven when I trudged into the house. I swung by the kitchen, poured a small scotch, and headed upstairs to bed.

The following morning, I woke before my alarm. With a

renewed vigor for work, I showered, dressed, and as spring appeared to have sprung, I walked the several blocks to the office. I phoned Sage on the way, but she didn't answer. I left a voicemail telling her how much I missed her already, uncaring whether that made me seem needy or desperate. I *was* needy *and* desperate.

Smiling at the receptionist who beamed at me and gushed a welcome back, I took the elevator up to the top floor of the ROGUES New York offices. Everything looked the same, yet different, but hell, it felt good to be back. Three months was a long time to spend cast out into the cold, but I'd learned my lesson. I couldn't allow my obsession over Athena's abduction to overtake my responsibilities to this company. The only obsession I might let get in the way, just a little, was the one I had for Sage.

"Gah, finally!" My executive assistant, Debbie, rose to her feet, arms outstretched. We hugged. Debbie, like most of the EAs around here, had been with me for years. She ran my life, and even during my enforced break, she'd still arranged my dry cleaning and sent over regular food parcels just in case I wasn't eating properly.

"I've missed you."

"Let's see if you still think that after I've bitten your head off for the fourth time."

She flicked her wrist. "I can handle you."

I chuckled. "Yes, you can."

"In all seriousness, I'm so glad you're back, Elliot. It's been strange around here without you." She kicked back her head. "There might be a little welcome gift for you in there. You go and get settled. I'll make you a coffee."

"Can you grab me a ham-and-cheese bagel from that place around the corner as well? I haven't eaten yet."

"And so it begins." She grinned. "I'd be happy to."

I pushed open the door to my office, and a huge cheer went up. Not that I could see anyone through the hundreds of helium balloons covering every available space. I batted a few to the side, revealing my five best friends, and suffered through a repeat performance of yesterday with lots of back-slapping and broad grins, but finally, they left me alone to settle in. When Debbie returned with my breakfast, I suggested she have someone gather up the balloons and take them to the children's hospital. It seemed wrong for them to go to waste—and besides, I kept having to whack them out of my way every five minutes.

The week flew by, despite me only snatching a single two-minute phone call with Sage. I understood how all-consuming her job was, but as I walked into my empty house on Friday, loneliness enveloped me. Mom had invited me over for dinner, but I'd declined. I wouldn't be good company, and anyway, I felt dog-tired. Using my brain in that way after an extended sabbatical had pushed me to the point of exhaustion. An early night would bring tomorrow along quicker, and Sage had agreed to stay over which meant... Sunday morning sex.

I changed out of my suit into an old pair of sweatpants and a baggy T-shirt, and shoved a frozen lasagna in the oven to heat. I poured a glass of wine while I waited and mused whether it was warm enough to sit on the roof terrace. Probably not. I should've moved to a new house by now, but after finding the perfect penthouse near to Oliver's place, the sale had fallen through, and my realtor hadn't found anything else suitable yet. In some ways, I'd be sad to leave this house. In others, I couldn't wait to move on to the next phase of my life. The one I planned to spend with Sage.

I had it all figured out. I'd booked a table at my favorite restaurant for eight o'clock tomorrow and, over fine food and the perfect wine pairing, I planned to ask Sage to move in with me. I'd thought about it a lot, and although some might think we were moving too fast, I disagreed. When you knew, you knew. And I'd find somewhere close by wherever we ended up for her mom and sister, too. Sage wouldn't leave them over in Brooklyn, and whatever made her happy, made me happy.

And if she outright rejected me...

No. I refused to even contemplate that outcome.

I made a mental note to introduce Sage to my realtor. If she was going to live somewhere, she should get a say in where that was and what it looked like.

The timer on the oven dinged. As I crossed the room, someone knocked on the front door. I rolled my eyes. This would be Athena coming by to check up on me after Mom told her I'd turned down a Friday night family gathering over at my parents' place. I switched off the oven, left the lasagna keeping warm inside, and went to answer the door.

"Surprise!"

My chin almost hit the floor. Sage, in full cop's uniform, stood on my front doorstep, arms thrown out wide, and a huge grin on her face.

"I'm on my break, so what better to do with an hour off than... you."

Chapter Twenty-Two

ELLIOT

"Fuck me," I ground out, clasping her wrist to pull her through the front door.

"That's the plan."

She giggled, and the sound went right to my dick, hardening me immediately. I had to maneuver around her utility belt to encircle her waist.

"I thought I wasn't going to see you until tomorrow," I groaned, pressing my lips to her neck.

She angled her head to the side. "It's been a crazy week. God, I love having my neck kissed."

"I know." I drew back and cupped her face. "Let's go upstairs."

"I don't have a lot of time."

"I'm a master of fast orgasms, both giving and receiving."

She laughed again. "I'll hold you to that."

We scampered up the stairs, and, given the shortness of time, I pushed open the door to the first bedroom I happened upon. I couldn't remember the last time I'd been in here, but there was a bed and sheets. We didn't need anything else.

I'd underestimated how much gear Sage wore when on duty, and it took longer than expected to liberate her from it all. Finally, we fell onto the bed in a tangle of arms and legs, mouths and tongues, and raw, ravenous need. Five days had passed since I'd touched her, but it felt more like five weeks.

She was ready, so ready for me. I sank into her wet heat, and an explosion of pleasure kicked up my spine and my balls tightened. Sage angled her hips and met me thrust for thrust. Resting back on my haunches, I lifted her ass and rubbed her clit, both of us watching as my solid length slid in and out of her.

"Damn, we look good," I said.

"So hot. Faster."

I did as she asked, and seconds later, her walls rippled around my cock, and I was done for. I squeezed my eyes closed and rode out the intense pleasure, then eased out of her and flopped onto the mattress, my heart thundering against my ribcage. I checked my watch.

"I think that's a new record." Moving onto my side, I played with her tits. "Tomorrow I plan to take my time."

She rolled over until we were face to face. "I missed you this week."

I pecked her lips, savoring the faint taste of mints. "I missed you, too. So damn much. Have you heard from Lily?"

Her entire face brightened. "Yes. Mom and I spoke to her on Tuesday and Thursday. She is having the most amazing time."

"I'm glad she's enjoying it."

"Thanks to you. How was your first week back at work?"

"Tiring, but good." My stomach growled, and I groaned. "Oh, fuck. I left a lasagna in the oven. It'll be ruined by now. Guess I'm ordering takeout. I don't suppose you have time to join me?" I added hopefully.

She shook her head and picked up my wrist to check the time. "In fact, I need to go soon." She flung her legs over the side of the bed and sat there for a moment, almost as if she was trying to muster the energy to go back to work.

I traced each vertebra of her spine with the tip of my finger. "A few more hours, a night's sleep, and then I have you for the entire weekend."

She twisted around and looked over her shoulder. "I can't wait."

Releasing a long, drawn-out sigh, she wearily got to her feet and dressed. She strapped on her utility belt and checked her gun. I wasn't a fan of firearms, but the idea of her drawing that thing and protecting herself or other members of the public got me hard again. Thankful for the room in sweatpants, I dressed, too. My shoulders drooped as we set off downstairs. I didn't want her to go, and she couldn't stay.

We hovered by the front door, neither one of us willing to open it and say goodbye. Several kisses later, Sage breathed out heavily. "I have to go."

"I know."

I reached for the door to open it, but before I even gripped the handle, someone knocked, one of those tentative knocks that smacked of a door-to-door sales agent who expected a rude welcome. I drew back the door. Helen, my birth father's wife, stood outside, one eye swollen shut, a split lip, and she was cradling her left arm across her chest.

Sage gasped. "Oh my God, Helen. What's happened?"

I ground my jaw to dust. I knew *exactly* what had happened. Leopards never changed their spots.

"He did this, didn't he?"

A strangled sob burst from Helen's throat. Sage flashed me a hard look, then elbowed me out of the way and helped Helen inside. She took her to the living room off the hallway and carefully settled her into a chair.

"Do you have a first-aid kit?"

I nodded and strode to the kitchen to fetch it. By the time I returned, Sage had helped Helen out of her coat and was on the radio, presumably to her precinct. I heard the words *domestic violence* and *assault* and a few others. They questioned the need for backup. Sage assured them she had it in hand.

"Should we call for an ambulance?" I asked, handing the kit over to Sage.

"No!" Helen exclaimed. "I don't want to go to the hospital. It's just a few bruises. I'll be fine in a day or two."

Yeah, Mom had avoided going to the hospital many times, too. Afraid of the questions that would arise, and the ultimate punishments he'd dole out because of the authorities getting involved. It was only on that last time, when he'd almost killed her, that she'd plucked up the courage to give a statement to the police.

A thought occurred to me, and I stiffened. "Where's Thomas?" *Dear God, don't let her have left him with that madman.*

She smiled, then winced when her lip split open further. "You remembered his name. He's at a friend's house. A sleepover."

At least that was something.

"What brought this on?" I asked.

Sage ripped open a packet of alcohol swabs. "Elliot," she castigated. "The questioning can wait, okay?"

"It's fine," Helen said. And then she hissed loudly as Sage dabbed a swab to her lip.

"Sorry. It'll sting a bit. I just need to clean it up so I can see if you need stitches."

I paced while Sage took care of Helen's injuries. This woman and her son were nothing to me, yet inside, I simmered with rage, my nails digging into my palms enough to draw blood. That used to be my mom sitting there with her face bashed in, trying to put a brave face on things for the sake of me and Athena. And now, more than a quarter of a century later, here we were, history repeating itself with another innocent woman he liked to use his fists on.

"Elliot."

Sage touched my arm, and only then did I realize she'd finished tending to Helen and had joined me on the far side of the living room. "I think a brandy might be a good idea. For the shock."

I nodded. "Is her arm broken?"

"It doesn't seem to be. Just sprained. I'd prefer she get checked out by a doctor, but she's adamant she won't go to the ER."

"I want to kill him."

She touched my face. "I'm sure this is bringing back terrible memories for you, but right now, let's concentrate on Helen and what she needs. Stay calm."

An impossible task, but I forced a reassuring smile anyway and went to get the brandy. I poured a decent amount in a glass and handed it to Helen, then took the seat beside her. She sipped and made a face.

"Tastes like medicine." She put it on the end table and then laid her limp hands in her lap.

"Ready to tell me what happened?" I asked, my voice a little on the curt side, evidenced by Sage's warning squeeze of my shoulder as she stood to my side.

Helen met my gaze, her eyes watery and mingled with confusion, hurt, and fear. "I told him I'd been to see you, to ask for help for Thomas. He went crazy."

"I'll bet he did," I muttered. "Did you know he beat my mom?"

She nodded. "When we met, he told me all about his past life. About you and your sister, your mom, and his stretch inside. He said prison changed him, and he wanted to build a new life with me. We were happy the first few years. Thomas came along, and he truly believed this was his second shot at fatherhood." Her chin lowered to her chest. "Then Thomas got sick, and I spent so much time in the hospital by his bedside, I think Tony felt powerless. That's when he began to hit me. At first, he was so contrite, so apologetic, but as time went on and Thomas's illness got worse..." She rubbed the space between her eyebrows. "He was angry all the time, or so it seemed to me."

"There is help out there," Sage said. "I can put you in touch with agencies who will support you."

She shook her head. "I love my husband. I don't want to leave him."

"Even when he uses you as a punching bag?" I bit out. "What kind of life is that? And have you even considered the effect this has on Thomas? Because trust me, he's taking it all in."

"I don't expect you to understand."

My nostrils flared, and I breathed out noisily. "Oh,

believe me, I understand all too well. If you love your son, you'll put him first."

"I do put him first," she exclaimed. "That's why I came to you the other day."

"Prove it. Walk away, if not for yourself, then for the damage that staying is doing to your son."

"Elliot!" Sage fired off a warning glare for me to dial it back. "You know things are never that cut and dried. Stop berating her."

I paced over to the fireplace and braced my hands on top of it.

"What's wrong with Thomas?" Sage quietly voiced the question I probably should have asked.

"His kidneys are failing."

I flexed my jaw. Christ. The poor little bastard. What a crappy pack of cards to live with. A wife-beater for a father, and a body fighting against him. In another life, that might've been me. And then I'd never have had the chance to meet Sage.

I cast a glance at the amazing, tough, beautiful woman tending to another woman who'd suffered more than enough for one lifetime, and now had to contend with the possibility of losing a child, and I voiced the decision I'd already made.

"I'll help," I said. "Forget what I said on Sunday. I'll cover his medical bills, whatever he needs."

Her bleak eyes met mine. "The medical bills aren't an issue. They were initially, when Thomas first became sick, but then we had a stroke of luck." She shrugged. "Just over four years ago, we won the state lottery. At first, I thought money would solve everything, but unfortunately for Thomas, all the money in the world won't help him. It's a kidney transplant he needs. That's why I came to you. To ask if you'd agree to get tested to see if you're a match. You and your sister. You're my last hope. Our last hope. Neither me nor Tony are a match for him."

A prickle of unease tingled at the base of my spine, and an instinct, honed over years of battling inside the corporate world, nudged at me, urging me to ask the question I feared the answer to.

"How much money did you win?"

A wry smile touched her lips. "Fifty million dollars. Amazing, huh?"

Fifty million dollars. The exact amount of Athena's ransom demand.

The truth came at me in a rush of horror and revulsion, sending me lurching to my feet. I spun to face Sage. At first, her brow wrinkled in confusion, and then the same realization I'd had hit her. She blindly reached for me. I pulled back.

"Where do you live, Helen?" I barely recognized the hoarse tone to my voice.

Sage pushed to her feet. "Elliot, don't."

"What's wrong?" Helen frowned. "What did I say?"

"Address," I gritted out. "Now."

She stammered out an address in Dumbo, Brooklyn. Sage made another grab for me. I shook her off. Snatching up a set of car keys from the hall table, I ran outside with Sage right behind me. She caught up to me as I opened the door to my Aston. She launched forward, but I was too quick. I threw myself into the car and locked the doors. The memory of Athena collapsed on the front step of my parents' house after that bastard released her crammed into my mind, sent blistering rage speeding through my bloodstream. I'd kill him. I'd fucking kill him.

She banged on the window. "Elliot, please. Don't do this."

I fired up the engine, and without sparing her another glance, I floored the gas pedal. The tires squealed on the asphalt, sending a cloud of smoke into the air.

The time for a reckoning had arrived, and I was going to make that bastard pay.

Chapter Twenty-Three

SAGE

I PATTED MY POCKETS. *DAMMIT!* MY KEYS WERE inside the house. My heart hammered against my ribcage as I ran back inside. *This is bad.* His father kidnapped his own daughter and extorted money from his son. My brain struggled to reconcile such a horrific idea, although we didn't have hard evidence, just Helen's inadvertent confession. It could be a coincidence, but I didn't believe in them. The timing fit, as did the amount of money they'd supposedly won.

"Stay here," I barked at Helen. "Don't go anywhere. I'll be back."

"What's happening?" Helen called out, but I had no time to explain. If I didn't catch up to Elliot, I feared what he'd do. His anger over his father and Athena's kidnapping fizzed along a precipice at the best of times. Now that those two events had collided, Elliot was a loose cannon, out of control. I had to stop him from doing something stupid, or risk losing him forever.

I dove inside my police vehicle and switched on the siren.

My car couldn't match an Aston for speed, but at least I had the benefit of being able to cut through traffic and jump any red lights. I was only two minutes behind him. With any luck, I'd arrive right after he did.

As fortune—or misfortune—would have it, the roads were surprisingly clear, and apart from skipping through one red light, my eyes darting everywhere as I crossed the intersection, I didn't get held up. Which meant Elliot hadn't either.

"Work with me, God," I muttered.

Arriving at the address Helen had choked out, I spied Elliot's car with the engine still running and the drivers' door wide open. I skidded to a halt and turned off the siren that he and his father couldn't have failed to hear. Something I hoped benefited me. I diverted to Elliot's car, grabbed the keys from the ignition, and locked it, then sprinted up the pathway.

The front door had clearly been forced open. I entered the property, raised voices reaching me. Unsure what I'd find, I drew my service weapon and, with my arms straight out front, I followed the commotion.

Please don't do anything stupid.

I came upon the two men, and my heart plummeted. The man I presumed to be Elliot's birth father was standing on the left-hand side of the room, a couch between him and Elliot, and, like me, he had a gun.

Pointed straight at Elliot's chest.

"Drop the weapon," I called out, bringing the man's head briefly around to me.

He jerked his gaze back to Elliot, the Glock in his hand as steady as any cop. This man knew how to fire a gun. It was right there in his stance and his unwavering aim. Fear for

Elliot thickened my throat. *Breathe, Sage.* This wasn't the time to let my personal fears cloud my professional judgement. I had to treat this like any other scene where I happened upon a man aiming a gun at an unarmed individual.

"Shoot him." Elliot fired me a sideways glance, then snapped his gaze back to his father. "Do it, Sage." He showed no sign of nerves or worry for himself, only an all-consuming hatred for the man standing opposite him pointing the barrel of a gun right at his chest. Fear had a scent, yet Elliot exuded nothing but penetrating focus.

"Put down the gun," I ordered without responding to Elliot. "No one needs to get hurt."

"Yes, they do," Elliot snapped. "He needs to. He kidnapped Athena. His own fucking daughter!"

"I know," I said gently. I had to defuse this situation. His father's finger kept twitching on the trigger, and Elliot looked set to launch at any second, his thighs coiled like a panther patiently waiting to take down his prey.

"Why'd you do it?" Elliot asked. "You abducted your own daughter. What kind of sick fuck are you?"

His father jabbed a finger on his free hand at Elliot. "After they released me from prison, I came to you for help, and you tossed it back in my face. What would a million bucks have been to you, huh? Nothing. It would have set me up nicely, but you loved it, didn't you? You *loved* telling me to fuck off. Loved the power you had over me."

"What did you expect?" Elliot hollered. "You deserved everything you got and more. I'd see you starving on the streets and I'd kick you in the balls as I walked past. *That's* how much I hate you."

"Let's all calm down."

Neither man paid me a moment's attention, their venomous gazes trained on each other.

"I threatened to cut off her finger. Did she tell you that?"

His father's voice came out eerily calm, and a tremor of fear raced up my spine, prickling across the back of my neck. I didn't like this. Not one bit. The only reason to tell Elliot something so horrific was to manipulate him. To provoke him into launching an attack that warranted an act of self-defense. I felt as if we were in the eye of a hurricane, waiting in the calm, knowing that any second, the winds would whip up and send hellfire raining down.

"Don't listen to him, Elliot. Listen to me. Listen to my voice."

It was as if I hadn't spoken. Elliot kept his focus on his father, his mouth clamped into a firm line. I dropped my gaze quickly to his hands fisted by his sides, the knuckles frighteningly white.

"I would have done it, too, if you hadn't paid up when you did." He laughed mirthlessly. "Imagine your face when you opened that package."

With a roar, Elliot launched forward.

The gun went off, piercing my eardrums.

I fired my weapon, aiming for his father's shoulder. It was completely against protocol, but something inside me yelled that if I deployed shoot-to-kill policy, I'd rob Elliot of his chance for justice.

Elliot's father cried out, and he collapsed, clutching his shoulder. He dropped the gun, and it scattered across the floor and disappeared underneath an end table. Elliot staggered backward.

"Are you okay?" I screamed at him as I sprang across the room, landing on top of the injured man. "Elliot!"

Yanking my handcuffs from my belt, I snapped them around his wrists. I read him his rights, hauled him to his feet, and reached for my radio.

"Sage."

I whirled around. Elliot's eyes were on me, his pupils dilated, his face morphed into shock, his hand clasped to his chest. And that was when I saw it. A rapidly spreading red stain, darkening his white T-shirt. He peered down at himself and then up at me, and then he collapsed.

"Elliot!"

I vaulted the couch and fell to my knees, pressing the flat of my hand on the wound, but the blood instantly seeped through my fingers. I snatched a blanket draped over the back of the couch and held it as tight as I dared to Elliot's chest.

"Stay with me, okay?"

His face grew deathly pale, and his lips tinged with blue.

"Don't you die on me, Elliot Bancroft. You hear me!"

I urgently spoke into my radio, calling for backup and medical assistance. Elliot's father weaved across the room and made a run for it.

"Elliot, please." Tears tracked down my cheeks, dropping onto the already sodden blanket coated in Elliot's blood. "You can't die. I love you. Fight for me, baby. Fight as hard as you can."

He didn't respond. I placed my ear next to his mouth. Warm air feathered my skin. *Yes!* Oh, thank God.

"Hold on, baby. Help is coming."

Sirens blared in the distance, edging closer, getting louder. Sobs racked my body, and thick, sticky blood coated my skin. He was losing too much. If they didn't get to him soon...

No!

He was young, fit, healthy, and a stubborn ass. He'd make it. He had to make it.

"Hello."

"In here," I cried, relief rushing through me at the sight of the paramedics, flanked by two cops. "Gunshot wound to the chest. He's lost a lot of blood. I've been compressing the wound."

"Good work."

One of them eased me out of the way while the other started setting up an IV. I blurted an abridged version of what had happened to the officers who immediately called it in. Elliot's father wouldn't get very far. Not handcuffed and with a busted-up shoulder. Even if the bullet had gone straight through the soft tissue and avoided hitting any bones, he'd be in a lot of pain and losing blood, too.

In minutes, the paramedics had Elliot loaded onto a gurney. I jogged beside them, holding his hand and muttering prayer after prayer. I couldn't lose him.

It only took ten minutes to arrive at the hospital. Somehow, Elliot was still clinging to life, although the shared worried looks between the two paramedics caused cold sweats to tear through my body. Surgeons greeted us and hurried him inside. A nurse took over from the paramedic, squeezing the fluids into his body. At any moment, he could go into cardiac arrest, or bleed out, or his organs might simply shut down. I clung to the hope that the bullet had only scraped his heart. If it had gone right through an artery, he'd be dead already. But that much blood indicated a serious injury.

Familiar with this particular hospital, I made it to the waiting area without my legs collapsing from underneath me. The place was packed to the rafters with Friday night drunks, screaming kids, and irate mothers. One kid stared at my bloodstained hands and pointed, then laughed. His mother scolded him, her voice low and rapid, then gripped his skinny little arm and yanked him into the seat beside her. The kid peeked around his mother. I smiled thinly. He stuck out his tongue. A giggle sneaked into my throat at the sheer normalcy in the middle of the worst day of my life, barring Lily's accident.

Please don't die, Elliot.

Tears tracked silently down my cheeks as I stared at the dried blood on my hands.

I should wash it off.

I didn't *want* to wash it off.

If Elliot didn't pull through, this was all I had left of him.

"Excuse me, Officer. Did you come in with the gentleman with the gunshot wound?"

I lifted my head and met the kind blue eyes of a doctor.

"Elliot," I whispered. "His name is Elliot Bancroft."

He nodded. "Are you his next of kin?"

Fear raced through me, stripping my mouth of every drop of saliva. If he was asking this, then... then...

"His girlfriend. Is he dead?"

"No."

I virtually collapsed, my body folding in on itself. I pressed my hand over my mouth. "Thank God."

"But his condition is very serious. He's lost a vast amount of blood. We're prepping him for surgery now, but as fast as we can get the blood into him, he's losing it. We have to move quickly and stop the bleeding."

"I'll call his parents and his sister. I should have called

them already." I patted myself down, looking for my phone. That I hadn't thought to phone them until now horrified me. "I need to call them."

He squeezed my shoulder. "I'll keep you informed."

I stared at his retreating back, and my eyes glazed over. I shook myself out of this frozen state and fished my phone out. Only then did it hit me that I didn't have Athena's number, or Ryker's. Nor their parents'. Goddamn it. I could call the precinct, but it'd take too long. I'd have to go through all the details. I needed someone who would act now and ask questions later.

Beth.

I brought up contacts and swiped the screen. Nothing happened. My sticky fingers wouldn't register. Fishing around in my pockets, I found a tissue. I dampened it and then wiped Elliot's blood off my right forefinger. Even losing that small amount felt like a betrayal, as if by ridding myself of his DNA somehow meant I was wiping him from history.

Strange, the thoughts that materialized when you were in shock.

I hit dial, my foot tapping as it rang out.

"Beth Tanner."

"Beth, I need a favor."

"Sage? What's wrong? You sound out of breath."

"I don't have time to explain. Can you locate someone for me and give me a contact number? I need it fast. Like now fast."

"What's the name?"

No messing, no preamble, no questions. God, I loved Beth.

"Athena Stone nee Bancroft. If you can't find her, look up Ryker Stone." I figured calling Athena instead of his parents was probably the best call, although this entire thing was just shit. I barely knew these people.

"Hang on."

The sound of tapping filtered down the phone line, and then she said, "Got it. I'll text over the details now."

"You're a lifesaver. Thanks, Beth."

I went to hang up when she shouted at me.

"Call me back when you have a minute, okay?"

"You got it."

I hung up and waited. Seconds later, an address and phone number landed in my text app. I breathed deeply to prepare myself for the terrible news I was about to drop and dialed.

Chapter Twenty-Four

SAGE

THE SOUND OF HEELS CLATTERING ON THE TILED floor brought my head up. Athena barreled toward me with Ryker a close second.

"Sage!"

She maneuvered around a few walking wounded, and I rose to greet her. She hugged me as if we were old friends. When she moved back, her cheeks were damp with tears. She looked me over, and then her eyes went wide.

"Is that... Elliot's blood?" She choked out a sob. "Oh, God."

"Where is he?" Ryker barked, his voice laced with all the authority I'd expect of a successful executive. "What the fuck happened?"

I squeezed my eyes closed, knowing that this wasn't my news to share, but I had no choice. I tugged on Athena's arm, pulled her down next to me. Ryker loomed over us both, his hand steady on his wife's shoulder.

"Are your parents on their way?"

Athena nodded. "They live farther out, but they should be here soon."

"Do you mind if we wait until then?"

"Yes, I do mind," Ryker snapped. "How the hell did he get shot, Sage? And what was he doing in Brooklyn?"

"Ryker, stop." She touched his hand. "It isn't Sage's fault. Shouting won't help anyone." She nodded. "We can wait."

He expelled a noisy breath, his nostrils flaring. "Have you had an update on his condition?"

"Not since the doctor told me they were prepping him for surgery."

"How long ago was that?"

"An hour. Maybe a bit longer."

"Not good enough. I'm going to find out what's happening."

He strode off.

"He doesn't mean to snap. It's an awful shock. How are you doing?"

Her kindness at a time when her brother teetered on the brink of death was my undoing. I covered my face with my hands and sobbed.

"Oh, Sage. Come here."

She wrapped her arms around my shoulders and gently rocked me while my heart shattered. When I gathered myself, she produced a pack of travel tissues and handed them to me.

"Here."

"Thank you." I removed one and blew my nose. "I don't know what I'll do if he doesn't make it."

"He'll make it, if only so he can brag to everyone that even a bullet can't finish him off." She rolled her eyes.

I laughed, and it felt good. It felt hopeful.

"Where's Ethan?" I asked, suddenly registering the absence of her and Ryker's son.

"He's with Oliver." When I stared blankly, she explained further. "He's a ROGUES board member. You met him at the baptism, but then, there were a lot of unfamiliar faces for you, so I'm not surprised you don't remember most of them."

"Yeah, it's all a bit of a blur."

Ryker returned five minutes later, his jaw clenched tight, and his lips thinned into a disapproving line. "They don't know anything, or if they do, they're not telling me."

"Why don't you see if you can find a vending machine?" Athena gently suggested. "Mom and Dad will be here soon. I'm sure they'd appreciate a warm drink."

Ryker stared at her, and it was as if they were silently communicating. "Fine."

I waited for him to leave. "How are you so calm?"

The faintest smile curved her lips. "Elliot's the hothead in our family. And besides, if I panic, Ryker will worry more about me than Elliot, and we should focus all our energies on him."

My chin wobbled, emotions I didn't know how to control fizzing to the surface. Fifteen years in the police force had taught me how to remain composed in the scariest of circumstances, yet as I tried to call on that training now, it failed me. All I could see was Elliot's pale face and blue lips, and the looks shared between the paramedics in the ambulance ride over here.

I swallowed down yet more tears. If Athena could hold it together, then I could, too. And besides, her parents would be here soon, and then I'd have to spill the entire awful tale of how he got shot. I wished I didn't have to do this. I wished Elliot hadn't gotten shot. I wished I'd driven faster and stopped him before he'd even entered that house.

"Mom!"

Athena scrambled to her feet and ran to greet her parents. She led them back over to the waiting area, and I received warm hugs from both these people who barely knew me yet offered comfort I couldn't say, hand on heart, I deserved. I kept replaying over and over how I might have stopped Elliot from driving off in the first place. Threw myself in front of his car, maybe.

Oh, hell. Helen.

I'd left her at the house. She wouldn't have a clue what had happened. There wasn't much I could do about that now. This was all such a mess, but I had to keep focusing on Elliot. Everything else would have to wait.

Ryker returned with coffees all around and, somehow, he'd wangled a family room where we could sit in peace and away from the craziness of the ER waiting area. As soon as the door closed behind us, the noise from outside abated and I could hear myself think. And I needed to think. Carefully. It was imperative I judiciously weighed each word before speaking.

"What happened, Sage?" Ryker kicked off the questioning, his brusque, forthright manner expressing his determination to gather the facts. *All* the facts.

I repeatedly rubbed my thumb over my wrist and tried to swallow, but the pain at the back of my throat stopped me. Without a clue on the exact place to begin, I started at the end.

"Elliot discovered who kidnapped Athena four years ago."

The whole room collectively gasped.

"Who was it?" Ryker crouched before me, a steeliness in his eyes. "Someone we know?"

I breathed in and switched my attention to Athena. I really had no clue how she would take this.

"It was your father. Your birth father, I mean."

"No." Athena's mom shot to her feet. "No, it can't be."

Athena paled and clasped at the silver necklace hanging around her neck. She scissored the pendant back and forth. "Is this true?" she whispered.

I nodded. "I'm so sorry. I wish you weren't hearing this from me."

Ryker took a seat beside Athena and gently placed an arm around her shoulders. I wasn't sure if he finally sat down because he feared the shock would take his legs from underneath him, or if he wanted to comfort his wife. Possibly both.

"But how did he find out?" Ryker asked. "After all these years. Every trail he followed went cold."

"I think you should ask Elliot once he recovers."

If he recovers.

I squeezed my eyes closed and dug my fingertips into my palms as more tears approached.

"I'm asking you." His voice, dripping ice, brooked no argument.

I blinked, and then glanced around, first at Athena and then her parents, Judy and Karl, hoping they'd back me up and agree we should hold off. If—no, when—Elliot came through his surgery, he'd want to tell them in his own way.

One look at their faces told me they were with Ryker on this one.

My stomach dropped to the cracked tiled floor at my

feet. I pulled my eyes away from Ryker's brooding stare and focused on Athena instead. I'd already started to think of her as a friend, and given the kind way she reached out and squeezed my hand in encouragement, I thought she might feel the same way. That she'd found it within herself to offer support to me when she must be reeling from shock was a testament to her character.

"A woman approached Elliot at the baptism on Sunday," I began tentatively, stumbling over the order of events while my enraptured audience leaned closer as if worried they might miss something important. "She asked for his help. Well, his and yours, actually." I gestured to Athena.

"Help with what?" Karl interjected.

Just say it. Get it over with.

"She introduced herself as Helen Carruthers and told Elliot she was married to his father."

I shot a glance at Judy. She swayed. Karl caught her, easing her into a chair.

"He remarried?" she whispered.

"It seems so. Elliot barely heard her out before he sent her packing. And then he told me in no uncertain terms that I wasn't to mention her visit to any of you." I lifted my right shoulder.

"That's why he was in such a foul mood when you both reappeared," Athena said. "I thought you'd had an argument."

"Oh, we did. Afterward."

"Gave him hell, huh?" She smiled faintly. "But I still don't understand. If all this happened on Sunday, how did he get shot tonight?"

"I stopped by Elliot's tonight while on a break from my shift." Heat filled my cheeks, and I ducked my head. *You can leave the next part out.* "Anyway, as I was leaving, Helen turned up again, out of the blue." I paused. "She had a black eye, a busted lip, and a sprained wrist."

Judy shook her head sadly, her shoulders wilting as if she carried a terribly heavy weight. "He still uses his fists, then. I knew he'd never change."

"She said that he'd been a good husband... until their son got sick."

"They have a son?" Athena gave up on the necklace and plucked at the soft skin at the base of her throat instead. "My half brother."

I nodded.

"And he's sick, you say?"

I nodded again.

"So that's what she wanted." Athena clenched her jaw. "Money."

"That's what Elliot thought at first. But tonight, she explained that her son, Thomas, has kidney disease. Like you said, Elliot is kind and generous, and he immediately offered to pay for all his medical treatment. Hearing that changed everything for him, despite his initial reticence to even speak to her." I glanced at each of them in turn. "And that's when the world fell in."

Ryker fidgeted in his chair, his patience clearly running out.

"She told him it wasn't money she needed. That right after their son got sick, they... won the lottery." I slowly blinked, and my gaze found its way to Ryker. "Fifty million dollars."

The truth hit him as hard as it had with Elliot, and he hissed through his teeth as Athena reached a shaky hand toward him.

"Oh my God," she whispered.

"Precisely," I said. "And Elliot obviously figured it out as fast as you just did. He ordered Helen to tell him where they lived, and before I could stop him, he took off. I gave chase. By the time I arrived, Elliot had busted down the door and your father had a gun pointed at him."

"And then he shot him?" Athena asked, her stare incredulous.

I could hardly blame her. If I hadn't witnessed the entire thing, I'd have struggled to absorb it, too.

"Not right away, no. I ordered him to drop his weapon. He refused, and then he began taunting Elliot, saying awful things." I pinched my nose to stave off an approaching headache. "It all happened so fast. Elliot leaped forward. The gun went off. I responded, and I hit his father in the shoulder, forcing him to drop the gun. At first, Elliot seemed fine, and I thought the bullet had missed, that Elliot launching at him had messed up his aim. I snapped handcuffs on your fa —the perpetrator. And then Elliot called my name, and that's when I saw the blood."

I covered my face with trembling hands. My body felt hot, my chest too tight to take a full breath.

Athena crouched in front of me and rested her hands on my knees. "He *will* be fine. He has to be." She gently gripped my wrists and tugged until I let my arms drop to my sides. "Listen to me. He'll survive. For you, he'll make it. I saw the way he looked at you on Sunday. I've never seen my brother look at a woman like that, ever. It was as if you were a dream and he couldn't quite believe his luck. Have faith, Sage."

I raised my head, seeking out Ryker. "Will you ask if there's any more news?"

His expression softened, and he stood. "You got it."

"I need to call my mom." I unsteadily got to my feet, waiting a few seconds for my head to stop spinning. "She'll be expecting me home tonight after my shift, and that's not going to happen."

I ducked out of the room and put in a quick call to Mom, giving her the abridged version. She made me promise to phone as soon as there was any news. My eyes welled with tears as I caught the worry and concern in her voice. I'd give anything to hug her right now, to feel her arms around me, and know that I could lose it, and all she'd do was hug me harder.

I finished talking to Mom, then I called Beth. There would be an inquest down the line, questions to answer on what I was doing operating in Brooklyn, outside my Manhattan jurisdiction, without backup, but the answers would have to wait. Until he was completely out of the woods, Elliot was my one and only priority.

Despite the late hour, she answered almost immediately.

"I'm glad you called back. What's going on?"

I gave her a brief update on the shooting as well as the bare bones of Helen's unexpected bombshell.

"Oh, Sage. How are you doing?"

"I'm okay." My voice cracked, and I cleared my throat. "Clinging on by my fingertips."

"Hang in there, honey. I'm here if you need anything."

"I do, actually."

"Shoot."

"Can you swing by Elliot's place and let Helen know what's happening? She won't be able to return home as the cops and forensics will be crawling all over the place, but if you can make sure she gets to somewhere safe, that'd be one less thing for me to think about. She has a child, although he's staying over at a friend's house, and she might prefer him to remain there tonight. She's a bit fragile, so go easy. I get the feeling she loves her deadbeat husband despite everything he's done."

"You got it. Text me Elliot's address and I'll take care of it."

"Thank you."

"What else can I do?"

"Find out whether the shooter is in custody. I doubt he'll have gotten far handcuffed and with a bullet in his shoulder, but I haven't told Elliot's family that his father bolted while I was tending to Elliot, and I need to know he's behind bars in case they ask."

"Done."

"And lastly... Try to calm my sergeant down. I know I'm in a heap of trouble for straying out of my jurisdiction without calling it in first, but I hoped I could fix things before they got out of hand." I laughed bitterly. "Safe to say I royally fucked that up."

"Don't worry about that right now. There's nothing we can't fix. Just concentrate on Elliot and yourself. Keep me updated."

"I will. Thanks, Beth. You're a lifesaver. I'll call you tomorrow."

I hung up, my gaze falling on Ryker walking my way. He shook his head. *No news.*

My throat constricted, and I squeezed my eyes closed, wishing this nightmare would end.

It was going to be a hell of a long night.

Chapter Twenty-Five

SAGE

My back spasmed, and I stiffly got to my feet and wandered over to the window. I parted the blinds, peering outside into the obsidian night, one that seemed to go on forever, torturing me and Elliot's family, leaving us in this perpetual limbo between life and death.

I checked my watch. Four oh five. I glanced around the room, meeting Ryker's tired gaze. Athena and her parents were sleeping, their bodies twisted at awkward angles in the uncomfortable chairs of the waiting room. At least we had quiet and privacy in here. I couldn't imagine spending all night out there with the masses, and people coming and going at all hours.

Ryker stood, stretched his arms overhead, then came to join me. Standing shoulder to shoulder, we silently prayed for the dawn of a new day, both of us undoubtedly hoping it brought the news we desperately wanted.

"Shall I see if I can rustle up coffee and maybe a snack?" Ryker asked.

I gave him a wan smile. "Coffee would be great. I don't think I can eat anything, though."

He gently squeezed my shoulder. "I'll fetch something anyway, just in case you feel like eating later."

With a loving glance at Athena, he quietly left the room. Less than five minutes later, he returned laden with steaming cups of coffee and a bag of pastries. He set everything down on the floor, then passed me a cup. I took it from him and blew across the top. He'd added cream, which I didn't usually take, but little details like that hardly mattered.

Athena stirred, groaning as she sat up. She rubbed her eyes.

"Here," Ryker said, passing her a coffee as well. "I got your favorite. Almond croissants."

The loving look she gave him caused a tightening across my chest. Elliot had looked at me like that right before Helen knocked and set in motion the tragic circumstances we were all now living through. It wasn't her fault, but that didn't stop me from wishing we'd never answered the door. Maybe if we'd still been in bed, we wouldn't have heard her, and...

Stop, Sage.

Longing for something that was impossible helped no one. Least of all Elliot.

A knock at the door jolted Judy and Karl awake, and when a doctor entered, both of them scrambled upright.

"Elliot Bancroft's family?"

"Yes." Judy wrung her hands.

I didn't move. If I did, I wouldn't make it far. Fear weighed on me, pressing down on my lungs, suffocating me as if there was a pillow covering my nose and mouth. Sweat trickled over the nape of my neck, and a knife twisted in my gut.

Be alive. Be alive. Be alive.

The doctor's lips moved, but the roaring in my ears meant I struggled to hear him. Judy sagged against Karl, as did Athena with Ryker.

It's bad. He's dead.

Tears rolled down my cheeks.

I'm going to throw up.

I stood and bent at the waist, and then my legs went out from underneath me. I cracked my head against the wall on the way down, but the pain there dulled when compared to the searing agony in my heart. This was my fault. I should have driven faster. I should have called for help. I should have saved him.

Athena's face swam in front of mine, worry drawing her eyebrows inward. She spoke but, as with the doctor, my brain couldn't convert the words into meaning. All I could do was stare at her blurry face and wait for the pain to cease.

"Sage."

She shook me lightly.

"Sage. He's okay. He made it through the surgery."

I blinked rapidly, a jolt of electricity sizzling through my veins. "What did you say?" I whispered.

"He's alive. He's going to be fine. They removed the bullet. He had to have several blood transfusions, but they've stabilized him, and they're happy he's through the worst."

I started to cry. Nothing silent about these tears. No, they were the ones that racked my entire body and left the men in the room highly uncomfortable while Judy and Athena, in women's solidarity, rubbed my back until I pulled myself together.

Face scrubbed of tears, I gingerly climbed to my feet in

case the bump on the head had resulted in a mild concussion. I managed to stay upright, and my vision was clear. A positive sign.

"Can I see him?" And then I bit my lip. His family should go in first. "Sorry. I mean after you've spent time with him, of course."

"Why don't we all go?" Judy suggested, giving me a motherly smile that made me hanker for my mom. She held out her hand. "Come on, sweetheart. I'm sure you're the one he really wants to see."

Warmth flooded my chest. These people didn't know me, not really, and yet here they were, opening their hearts and treating me like one of their own. Humbled, I pressed my palm to Judy's, and the five of us left behind the room we'd spent the last ten or so hours in and rode the elevator up to the fifth floor to Elliot's room. A doctor met us outside, warning us of the need for Elliot to rest and limiting our visit to five minutes.

As desperate as I was to see him, I held back, lagging behind his parents, his sister, and his best friend. The room reeked of antiseptic, that awful hospital smell that clung to your clothes and your hair, and no amount of washing seemed to get rid of it. I distinctly remembered the smell from Lily's accident, and it had never left me. All those awful memories came racing back, stealing the air from my lungs. I propped a shaky hand against the doorjamb and waited for the moment to pass. I couldn't see Elliot for the sea of bodies between me and him, and the constant beep from the machines monitoring his vital signs gave me the shivers.

A strangled sob broke from Judy's throat, and she stumbled across the room. "Oh, my baby."

"Mom, for Christ's sake," he rasped. "I'm thirty-fuck-ing-four."

I mightn't have a clear line of sight, but hearing his voice sent relief barreling through me. If he could muster the energy to scold, then maybe he really would be okay. I couldn't wrap my brain around it. One minute, I'd feared I'd lose the love of my life before he even knew how deeply I felt about him, and the next, he was reprimanding his mother for fussing.

"You'll always be my baby," Judy continued, unfazed by his rebuke.

"The things you'll do to get out of working. Lazy bastard." This from Ryker. "I called the guys. They're on their way."

"You had us so worried, Elliot," Athena said.

"Is Sage here?" he croaked.

Another tear squeezed out of the corner of my eye, despite rapid blinking to try to hold it back. The bodies parted, and my eyes locked on to Elliot, propped up against a stack of white pillows with wires stuck to his chest, and a white gauze bandage protecting the area where they'd oper-ated to remove the bullet.

"Hey, angel," he said. "Sorry I fucked up."

"Oh, Elliot."

I somehow got my feet working and staggered over to his bed. A chair appeared from nowhere, and I fell into it. Careful not to dislodge the needles in the back of his hand, I picked it up just so I could feel his warmth and prove to myself that he was very much alive.

"Guess I'm not immortal, huh?"

His dad let out a low chuckle. "Guess not."

Wincing, Elliot shifted his weight, and his eyes drooped. "Damn, I'm tired."

"We should let him rest," Ryker said, curving an arm around Athena's waist. "Now that we know he's going to be okay, I suggest we all go home, get some sleep, and come back later."

"Good idea." Judy leaned down and kissed Elliot's cheek. "We'll see you in the morning, sweetheart. Sleep well."

"Mmm," was all Elliot managed.

I didn't want to leave him, but our five minutes were up, and any second the doctor would arrive and kick us out anyway. I brushed my lips over his, but he'd already fallen asleep.

I'd left my squad car in Dumbo and traveled to the hospital in the ambulance with Elliot, so Ryker and Athena gave me a ride home. I trudged toward my building on legs that would give a newborn foal a run for its money. I expected to find the apartment in darkness. Instead, Mom was sitting up waiting for me. The second I saw her, I threw myself into her arms.

"Oh, Sage. How is he?"

"He's going to make it."

Mom expelled a deep breath. "Thank God."

I drew back. "I should shower and change."

"I'll make some coffee."

I removed my blood-soaked uniform and stood under the hot spray, washing away the horror of a night that had lasted longer than a month. At least that was what it felt like. Clean and dry, and swaddled in a bathrobe, I curled up on the couch next to Mom and sipped at my coffee. Forget those fancy baristas. No one made coffee like my mom. I finished the cup and set it on the coffee table.

"Why don't you get some sleep?" Mom suggested.

I shook my head. There was no way I'd be able to shut my mind down enough to fall asleep. "I need to go into work, Mom. I have things to do." Like find out what happened with Elliot's father, and face the music.

It wouldn't be pretty.

Chapter Twenty-Six
SAGE

I'D RECEIVED MY FAIR SHARE OF DRESSING DOWNS over my long tenure working for the New York Police Department, but even I couldn't deflect the metaphorical whipping doled out by my sergeant for the number of transgressions I'd made by chasing after Elliot. By the time he'd finished, I felt flayed alive. I must have apologized a hundred times, each one greeted with another tirade. I'd always known my sergeant was a fearsome dude, and he deserved every scrap of his reputation.

I left his office and bumped straight into Bryce. His hard, narrowed eyes sent a clear message: *I'm pissed off at you.*

"Abbott," he snapped. "You're alive, then."

"Severely battered and bruised," I said, forcing a quick grin. "Then again, you know the boss."

"I thought I knew you."

I lightly touched his arm. "I am sorry, Bryce. There just wasn't time to call you. It all happened so fast."

"You told me you had a quick errand to run on your

break and you'd be back soon. Then the next thing I hear is you've shot some dude over in Brooklyn, and despite several calls I made to your cell, you couldn't be bothered to return a single one."

He had a right to feel annoyed, betrayed even, but now *I* was salty. "Forgive me if you weren't at the top of my agenda, Bryce. I was busy worrying about the chances of my boyfriend surviving a gunshot wound to the chest. He's come through the surgery, thanks for asking."

Bryce palmed the back of his neck and had the good grace to look a little ashamed. "That's good," he mumbled.

"Yes, it is. Now if you don't mind, I have somewhere to be."

I shoved past him.

"Abbott?"

I pulled up but didn't turn around. "What?"

"Got time for a coffee later?"

My lips twitched. Bryce never could stay mad for long, and this was his way of apologizing for raining down on me when I'd already had a gutful from my sergeant.

I glanced over my shoulder. "Maybe. You're buying, and I'm going to order the most expensive thing on the menu."

He pointed his finger at me and winked. "You got it."

I went in search of Beth. Despite it being a Saturday, and not quite nine o'clock yet, there she was, sitting behind her desk, brow furrowed, poring over a thick file. Weekends meant nothing to Beth if she was trying to crack a case. She'd rather give her team more time off and work right through herself.

"Any news?"

She jumped. "Fuck, girl. Them's some silent feet you've got."

I chuckled, flopping into the chair opposite her desk. She closed the file.

"How's he doing?"

I smiled faintly. "He's going to make it."

"Oh, Sage, that's great. That's really great."

"Yeah, and once he's fully recovered, I'm going to kill him."

She sniggered.

"Have they got him?" I didn't need to expand. Beth knew exactly who I was referring to.

"Yes. They found him a quarter mile from his house. He's in the hospital under armed guard. You managed to miss hitting any bones, so he should be out today, and then they'll take him into custody."

My skin prickled. "Which hospital?"

"Brooklyn General."

I flexed my jaw. "Same hospital as Elliot."

"It's a big hospital, Sage," Beth said, correctly guessing the reason for my disquiet.

"Yeah, true."

"You'll need to give a statement. I'll text you the details of the officer in charge of the case."

"Thanks. I'll get right on it as soon as I've seen Elliot this morning."

"You look exhausted."

I wearily swiped a hand over my face, evidence her comment was on the money. "I got home around five-thirty this morning. Too late to try and sleep, so I showered, drank a gallon of Mom's coffee, then came in to face the music."

"Ah. Sergeant Rutherford a bit brutal, was he?"

"Brutal? I need skin grafts where he flayed me."

Beth chuckled. "You'll live."

"Yeah. It's character building. What about Helen?"

"She refused help. Last I heard, she'd turned up at the hospital demanding to see her husband."

I sighed deeply. I'd hoped she'd see the light, but in this case, it seemed as if love truly was blind. "That's her choice. We can only offer the helping hand. They have to find the courage to take it."

"True that. We've seen enough domestic violence victims return to their abusers. With any luck, one day, she'll see him for what he really is and reach out for the help that's waiting."

"I hope so. Thanks for everything, Beth. I appreciate the heck out of you."

"That's what friends are for."

"And I got a good one in you." I rose from the chair. "Maybe once this is over, we should have a girls' night out? Cass is always up for a night of drunken debauchery. As long as I give her enough notice she can make her way from upstate."

"Sounds like a plan."

I said goodbye to Beth. Now that I'd survived the dressing down from the boss, my steps were lighter as I walked the couple of blocks to the subway, and excitement at seeing Elliot grew. I called the hospital, and they told me he was still sleeping, but that his vital signs were stable and they were happy with his progress. Even if he slept all day, I just wanted to sit by his bed and hold his hand. To feel the warmth of blood circulating in his veins when the outcome could have been horrifically different.

When I arrived, he already had visitors. His mom and dad, and Ryker and Athena had beaten me to the punch, and sitting outside his room were a couple of the ROGUES board members, Oliver and Upton, if my memory served me from meeting them at Ethan's baptism this past Sunday. It hit me how loved Elliot was and how, if he hadn't made it, it would have affected so many lives.

I bit down on the ache that surged in my chest, reminding myself it was all moot. Elliot had beaten the odds and survived.

"He's been asking for you," Oliver—at least I thought it was Oliver—said, his smile friendly and warm.

I swallowed a lump of guilt that I hadn't been here when he'd woken up and pushed open the door to his room. The smile Elliot gave me when our eyes connected chased away all dark thoughts, lighting me up from the inside. He looked so much better than when I left him in the early hours of this morning. His face wasn't as pale, and he was far more alert.

Judy and Athena hugged me as if I belonged, and Karl gave up his seat by his son's bed for me. Elliot held out his hand, and I took it.

"Guys, do you mind giving us a few minutes? I want to talk to my girl alone."

My girl.

My heart just about exploded.

Without a murmur of dissent, they all nodded. Judy kissed Elliot's cheek and then slipped her arm through her husband's.

"We'll be back later, darling."

As soon as the door closed, my face crumpled. "I thought you were dead."

Sorrow tugged at the corners of his lips, and he patted the small space on the mattress. "Come here. I want to feel you next to me."

I somehow tucked myself into his side, being as careful as I could not to dislodge any wires or hurt him.

He kissed the top of my head. "I really am sorry I left like that."

"It's me who's sorry. I failed you. I never should have let him fire his weapon."

"No." He tilted up my chin. "Don't do that. You aren't responsible. *He* is. He chose to pull the trigger." His jaw flexed. "He's in custody, right?"

"Actually, he's... here."

Elliot's eyebrows shot north. "In this hospital?"

"Yeah. He's under armed guard, though," I rushed on to say. "And I believe they will release him today and take him straight into custody."

A nerve beat in his cheek. "At least he'll finally get what's coming to him."

"And what about you? Helen's innocent remark was such a shock."

He breathed noisily through his nose, his nostrils flaring, and he got that look in his eyes, the murderous one. "I'm good."

"I don't think you are. You haven't unpacked your grief, Elliot. It's still there, buried beneath the surface, showing itself in flashes of uncontrolled rage."

His chest rounded as he breathed deeply. "Do my folks know? Athena?"

Ah, they mustn't have told him I'd let them know the full story. "I had no choice."

He briefly glanced toward the window. "How is she?"

"Resilient," I said. "Your sister is quite a woman."

He turned back to face me. "Yes, she is."

"She was stunned, just like we were, but she was far more worried about you."

"She knows all about Helen, too?"

"Yes." I heaved a sigh. "I'm sorry, Elliot. I'd rather such monumental news came from you rather than me, but I didn't have a choice.."

"Hey."

He caressed my face, then belying the fact he'd spent hours in surgery, fighting for his life, he kissed me. I allowed myself a moment to savor him, but as he deepened our connection, I pulled back.

"No. You've had major surgery, and you lost a lot of blood."

"Not so much that I'm not hard for you right now."

"Elliot!"

He laughed and then hissed through his teeth. "Okay, laughing is off the table for a little while."

"So is sex."

He pouted, and I laughed.

"Sage?"

"Yeah?"

"All this." He gestured to his injury. "It's on me. Not you."

I ran a hand through his soft hair, anchoring it there to stop it shaking, aware I still felt the reverberations of what I'd nearly lost. "I was so scared, Elliot. I've seen my fair share of gunshot wounds, but when it's someone you love lying there, teetering on the brink of death, it's terrifying."

He stilled, apart from the rapid blinking of his eyelids. "You love me?"

Damn. I hadn't meant it to come out like that. Hardly the most romantic of ways. Then again, I'd never said those words to anyone except for Mom and Lily, and that wasn't the same at all.

I drew my top teeth across my lip and nodded. "Yes, I love you. My timing sucks. I wish I were telling you under different circumstances. You don't have to say it back."

His mouth curved down at the corners. "Okay."

That one word, thrown out there so casually, was a knife to my gut. Everyone's greatest worry was telling someone they loved them only to have them not say it back, and here I was, experiencing the ordeal first-hand.

"Maybe I should let you rest?"

His arm dropped from around me, allowing me to slip from the bed. I'd obviously scared him off. Why couldn't I have kept my big mouth shut? I bent to pick up my purse from the floor.

"Sage?"

I straightened but kept facing away from him. "Yeah?"

"Look at me."

I slowly pivoted, lifting my eyes to his, expecting to see regret, sorrow, or maybe disappointment. Instead, his eyes twinkled with mischief.

"I love you, too."

Realizing he'd teased me, and unable to throw something at him given his delicate state, I growled instead. "Elliot Bancroft, you are an asshole."

"I know. And you are adorable when you're angry."

Chapter Twenty-Seven

ELLIOT

"KNOCK, KNOCK."

Athena poked her head inside my hospital room, and I gratefully beckoned her inside. Three long days stuck in here, and I was teetering on the edge of insanity.

We'd only briefly discussed the elephant in the room, Athena insisting I rest up and get well before we dived head-first into the quagmire of knowing the man who fathered us had kidnapped his own daughter under the guise of extorting money from me. Even now that I'd had a few days to reflect on it, I still couldn't quite believe he was the man I'd spent more than four years searching for, and all this time he'd lived right on my doorstep in a home that my money paid for.

She pulled a chair up to my bedside. "I brought you these," she said, landing a bunch of grapes in my lap.

I laughed, and it only hurt a tiny bit. "Thanks, I think."

I plucked one off its stalk and popped it into my mouth. Athena helped herself to a couple as well, chewing thoughtfully.

"So, Sage told me he's been charged and refused bail on the basis that he intended to post bond with illegally gained funds, and that he posed a high flight risk."

"Good. I hope he rots."

Her mouth twisted to one side, and prickles crept across the back of my neck.

"What?" I asked.

"You always could read me like a book." She took a deep breath. "I want to see him."

"I hope you're fucking joking."

A faint smile touched her lips. "That's what Ryker said, but I'll tell you the same as I told him. I want to look him in the eye and ask him outright if he did it."

Her hand flew in the air as I opened my mouth.

"Yes, I *know* he did it, but I need to hear it directly from him. I put this behind me a long time ago, Elliot, unlike you. But that doesn't mean I never wanted closure. *This* is how I get it."

I chewed the inside of my cheek, really reflecting on what she'd said instead of my usual go-to of flying off the handle and ordering her never to see him.

Yeah, I could just imagine how that would go down with Athena.

I despised the idea of my sister getting within ten feet of that bastard, but I also understood her desire to look him in the eye and work out for herself something I'd known for a long time: that he wasn't worth shit and neither of us should give him any power over us.

"I won't make a fuss on one condition."

She narrowed her eyes, suspicion swirling in her amber irises, so like my own. "What?"

"That you let me come with you."

She pressed a hand to her chest and smiled. "I rather hoped you would. Can you talk to Sage? I'm not sure how we even go about visiting someone who's incarcerated."

"Yeah. She should be here shortly. She flies to Arizona tomorrow to pick up her sister, so I'm not sure she'll have time to arrange it before she leaves, but she might be able to put us in touch with someone who can."

Sage having to pick up her sister alone was another curse I laid at that bastard's door. I'd begged the doctor to release me so I could go with her to pick up Lily, but he'd told me no, and then doled out the shitty news that I'd be in here until Friday at the earliest. Debbie, my executive assistant, had arranged everything so Sage wouldn't have to worry, but I'd much rather escort her myself.

"Thank you." She pinched another grape and tossed it into her mouth. "There's something else."

I flopped my head against the pillow, anticipating further angst. "What now?"

A tap on the door prevented Athena from replying. The moment of irritation faded when Sage appeared.

"Oh, am I interrupting? Do you want me to come back?"

"No," Athena interjected before I could. "Actually, it's good timing that you're here."

She gestured for Sage to take the seat next to hers, and we broke the news regarding visitation in prison. Sage appeared surprised, but promised she'd have someone call us to arrange a time.

"You were about to drop another bomb," I said to Athena. "Hit me with it."

Her gaze rested on my face. She rubbed her fingertips over her lips. "I met Helen—and Thomas."

"Oh." I wasn't at all surprised Athena wanted to meet him. Knowing she had a half brother out there wasn't something she'd allow to lie. And I guessed I felt the same way. It wasn't Thomas's fault he had a shitty father any more than it was mine or Athena's, and I was curious about him.

"What's he like?"

"Smart, funny, cute. He looks a lot like you did at his age."

I pulled my lips to one side. "Helen said he needed a transplant."

Athena nodded. "His kidneys are failing. He's been on dialysis for more than four years now, but the doctors say if they don't find a donor within the next six months, it'll be over for him."

Sage gasped. "Oh God. How terrible."

"Fuck." I swept a hand over my face.

"Yeah." Athena nibbled the tip of her thumb. "They found out he was ill about three months before my... I was taken. I think that's why he did it, Elliot. The bills were piling up, and without the treatment, Thomas wouldn't have made it this far."

I ground my teeth and glared at her. "Don't you *dare* make excuses for him."

Sage closed her hand over mine, a caution to rein in my temper.

"I'm not. The way he dealt with it was cruel. Dreadful. But it helps me to think there's a reason rather than pure greed or wickedness."

"You're too kind, Athena. That's always been your problem."

"Problem?" Her lips formed a thin line. "I don't think being *kind* and *compassionate* is a problem, Elliot. And neither do you. But when it comes to him, you can't be objective."

"Do you blame me?" I asked.

"Maybe I should leave you guys to it," Sage said, getting to her feet.

"No, stay." Athena tugged on her arm until she retook her seat. "You'll have to get used to our bickering, Sage. It's always this way with us. But that's because my brother is a jerk."

Sage snickered. "On occasion, I concur with that."

"Oh great," Elliot said. "Where's Ryker when I need backup?"

"He won't save you," Athena said. "And if you've quite finished being snippy, there is something even more serious that I need to talk to you about."

"Then I absolutely should go," Sage said.

"No. This affects you, too." Athena rubbed her lips together. "I got tested. I'm not a match."

My pulse stuttered. "Then I'm his last hope."

"Yes."

My palm skimmed along my jaw. "This is fucking huge, Athena."

"I know. And you mightn't be a match either."

"And if I am..." I tailed off.

"You aren't under any obligation," Athena said. "We don't know these people, and we owe them nothing, but he's just a little boy, Elliot, and his whole future is at risk. I keep thinking if this was Ethan... I'd do anything to help my son. And that's all Helen is doing."

I sought out Sage. Her expression was unreadable. "What do you think?"

She blew out a breath, her cheeks puffing up. "That's a

tough question for me to answer, Elliot. On one hand, I really don't want you to do it. You've been through so much, and you have a long recovery ahead of you. A transplant operation would put even more strain on your body, and it wouldn't be able to take place for a few weeks either, I'd guess." She lowered her eyes and shook her head. "On the other hand, like Athena said, I think of Lily, or my mom, and I know I'd do anything to save them."

My insides twisted, a sense of dread mingled with courage—an odd combination—taking root in my stomach. There was no point worrying too much until I knew whether I was a match. And if I was, then I'd weigh all the options and decide on the right course of action for me, for Sage, and for my family first. Selfish? Maybe, but they were my priority, and like Athena said, we owed these people nothing.

"I'll arrange to have the relevant tests done. There's no point speculating on what I may or may not do until I know whether I'm a match."

"That's a good idea," Athena said, although Sage looked far less convinced.

I clasped her hand, drawing on her strength and warmth. "I wish I was coming to Arizona with you."

"I do, too, but I'll only be away one night."

I lifted her hand to my lips and kissed it. "Longest night of my life."

Chapter Twenty-Eight

ELLIOT

THE DOCTOR SHUFFLED A STACK OF PAPERS ON HIS desk, then opened a brown file and scanned the contents. "I have the results back."

Sage gripped me tighter, her hand almost crushing mine. I flexed my fingers beneath hers, and she eased off about ten percent.

"And?" I queried, my gaze locked on the doctor.

"You're a match."

I nodded, unsurprised. Weirdly, I'd expected this outcome. "Well..." I glanced over at Sage, her face ashen. "Now we know."

The room fell silent, and the doctor, picking up on the tension bouncing off the walls, cleared his throat, then pushed his chair back from his desk and got to his feet.

"I'll give you two some time alone to discuss things."

The door closed with a quiet click, and I shifted in my seat. "Talk to me. Tell me what you're thinking."

"I'm thinking that I don't want you to do it, Elliot. God, I hate myself for saying that, but it's how I feel. This isn't donating blood, or plasma, or even something like bone marrow. This is giving away one of your organs in a major operation that will take you weeks to recover from. I won't lie to you. I'm struggling with the idea of it."

"I don't want you to lie to me. I always want to hear what you're honestly thinking. But I've been thinking, too. A whole lot. Athena wants to visit him in prison because she's decided that's how she'll get closure. Me? That won't give me closure. I've seen him already, and I can say with certainty that won't work for me. But this... the ability to save Thomas... maybe that's how I finally put the past behind me and move on. I'll never be able to forgive *him* for the terrible things he's done. Beating my mom, kidnapping Athena, shooting me. But—and this is probably going to sound awful—by saving his son, a son he'll barely see from the prison walls I'm determined he'll spend the rest of his life behind, it kind of feels like I've won. I've taken the high moral ground and proven I'm a better man than he could ever hope to be."

She took a breath and let it out slowly. "I almost lost you. The idea of you volunteering to go under the knife, to put your body through another huge surgery... it terrifies me, Elliot."

I rested a hand on her thigh. "I'm scared, too. This is such a huge decision, and I need to find out more about the procedure, the risks, and the recovery time before I can commit to it. But I need you by my side, angel. You're my strength... and my weakness. If, once we've uncovered the facts, you still don't want me to do it, then I won't. My future lies with you, and that means you'll always come first. Today, tomorrow, forever."

She curved her hands around my face and bent her head,

brushing her lips over mine. "I love you, and I'll support you in whatever you decide. I would never demand you make a choice like that. Let's talk to the medical staff and then we can go from there."

"Shall I call the doctor back inside?"

She gave me a wry smile. "No time like the present."

———

I dropped my keys on the hall table and trudged into the living room. Sage followed, and the two of us collapsed onto the sofa. She leaned her head on my shoulder, and we sat in silence, staring at the wall. The doctor had given us both a lot to think about, but despite the risks that came with being a live organ donor, a voice deep inside my head kept telling me this was the answer. *This* was how I finally let go of the hate and the anger that I'd carried inside me for far too long. Without acknowledging it, I'd allowed the man who'd spawned me far too much power, and it had poisoned my life for long enough. I had so much to look forward to and a bright future with the woman I loved, but if I didn't go ahead with this and Thomas died, as he undoubtedly would, I knew it would taint our lives. I'd never truly forgive myself for letting an innocent child wither away when I could have done something to save him.

"I think I should call Helen and ask her if I can meet Thomas." I kissed the top of her head. "I don't think I can make a final decision unless I see him."

She craned her neck, her worried gaze colliding with mine. "If you meet him, you'll go through with it."

I pulled in my lips. "Probably."

Expelling a heavy sigh, she nodded. "I think you've already decided, Elliot. This is just the rubber stamp."

"Will you forgive me?"

She shifted her position, drawing her legs up onto the sofa and crossing them. "There is nothing to forgive. I'm lucky to have found such a kind, compassionate, caring man to spend my life with. I told you I'd support whatever choice you make, and it sounds to me like you've made it."

I traced a fingertip along the inside of her thigh. "Nine days ago, I planned to ask you to move in with me, but then I went and got myself shot and all." I shrugged, then grinned. "So, better late than never, will you?"

Her eyes widened. "Move in here? With you?"

I laughed. "Yes, with me. And, here for now. I've been looking for a new place for a while. But you get to choose where we live."

"Oh, Elliot." She ran her gaze over me, her eyes soft and warm. "I want nothing more, but I can't leave Mom and Lily."

"I wouldn't expect you to. Wherever we choose will be more than big enough for them, too, or if your mom would rather have her own place, then I'll buy her one close by."

"You can't do that. Besides, Mom would never take that kind of charity."

I raised my eyebrows. "It's not charity, angel. It's what you do for family." I chuckled. "It's not as if I won't be getting what I want. Which is you, in my bed, every night. I want to wake up beside you and have morning sex and shower sex and bend-you-over-the-kitchen-table sex."

She arched a brow. "Maybe we shouldn't suggest Mom and Lily live with us then. My mom is very broad-minded, but I'm sure she'd rather not see that."

I laughed again. "Say yes, Sage. Say yes and make me the luckiest man alive."

My heartbeat kicked up a notch as I waited for her answer. She tucked a stray strand of hair behind her ear and then nodded.

"Yes."

"Goddamn." I snapped a hand around the back of her neck and yanked her toward me, kissing her hard. "I fucking love you, and as soon as these stitches are out, I'm gonna throw you over my shoulder, carry you upstairs to bed, and screw you all night long."

She batted her eyelashes at me. "It's that kind of sweet talk that sealed the deal."

———

A tentative knock on the door propelled me to my feet. I shot a glance at Sage, then Athena, who'd agreed to be here to provide moral support, and as a familiar face for Thomas, seeing as she'd met him twice now.

"Guess that's them."

Sage nodded. "I guess." When I stood there, feet frozen to the carpet, she flicked her wrist. "Well, don't leave them standing outside."

I wiped my hands on my jeans. "Is it weird that I'm nervous?"

"No," Athena said. "You're about to meet your half brother. That's huge. But you're going to adore him, Elliot. He's a super kid."

I walked into the hallway and dampened my lips as I stood in front of the door. With a deep breath, I opened it and barely contained my shock. Athena wasn't joking when she said he looked a lot like I had at his age. The only difference was his eyes were brown rather than the amber eyes Athena and I had. But apart from that, he resembled me as a child.

"Hi." I smiled at Thomas, then flicked my gaze to Helen. Her bruises had faded in the eleven days since she'd turned up on my doorstep and dropped a bombshell I still struggled to absorb.

She returned my smile with a cautious one of her own. "Hi, Elliot." She curved an arm around her son's shoulder. "This is Thomas."

He beamed. "Mommy tells me you're my brother. Does that mean Athena is your sister, too?"

I crouched and ruffled his hair. "It does. She's here. Would you like to come in and say hello?"

"Sure."

He hopped inside, full of confidence. I found myself a little taken aback. Somehow, I'd expected him to look pale and ill, and maybe clinging to his mother, given the enormity of the changes to his life. Yet he appeared well. He wasn't underweight, his cheeks were rosy, and his eyes glowed.

"He's often like this right after his dialysis," Helen murmured. "He gets a brief burst of energy, and then he'll start to feel unwell again."

"Oh. I see."

I led them through to the living room. He hugged Athena, and I introduced him to Sage then held out my hand. "How about a tour of the house, buddy?"

There wasn't much here that a ten-year-old would find all that interesting, but I thought a little alone time, just me and him, might be good for both of us.

"Sure," he repeated.

I passed over most of the rooms and headed up to the roof terrace.

Thomas ran over to the railings and peered over. "This is neat."

"Yeah, I like it." I sat on one of the chairs and held my face up to the sun. "Why don't you come and sit down."

"Okay." He skipped over and flopped into the chair beside mine.

"Your mom tells me you're not very well."

"My kidneys don't work."

He stated the facts so baldly, his attitude matter-of-fact, that I blanched. "And does that stop you from doing stuff? Stuff that kids do like running and riding your bike and playing outside with your friends?"

"Yeah." He bit his lip. "It sucks sometimes. I get tired a lot."

My chest ached, and not from the surgery. "What would it mean to you if you could do all those things?"

A broad grin spread across his face. "There's this huge tree near my house. I'd climb it. Right to the top."

"And what would you do when you got there?"

He shrugged, almost as if he hadn't thought about the endgame, only the journey. "I'd watch all the people walking by. They wouldn't know I was there."

"No, they wouldn't."

"Did you used to climb trees when you were my age?"

"I did all kinds of things," I said. "I was always getting into some mischief or other."

"You're lucky," he said.

My emotions rushed to the surface, and I almost cried for this kid. He'd been dealt so many shitty cards, I had no idea how he'd stayed so normal, so positive. I'd already made the decision to go through with the operation, but these past few minutes had strengthened my resolve. In saving Thomas, I'd save myself.

"Shall we go and see what your mom is up to?"

"Can I come here again?"

I held out my hand, and he took it. "Buddy, you can come here whenever you want."

We returned to the living room. Helen's gaze fell to where Thomas and I were joined, and her eyes, filled with hope, were also tinged with apprehension.

"Thomas, how about we see what flavors of ice cream Elliot has in his freezer?" Athena asked.

"Do you have chocolate?"

Athena glanced at me. I shrugged. There could be anything in there. Or nothing.

"Why don't we go check it out and see," she suggested.

"Okay," he replied, good-naturedly, bouncing alongside her.

As soon as he was out of earshot, Helen turned to me, her fingers plucking at the hem of her sweater.

"Have you gotten the results back?"

"Yes."

Her breath hitched, and she wrapped both arms around her stomach. "It's bad news, isn't it?"

"I'm a match."

She gasped and tears welled up. They clung to her lashes for a few seconds, then tracked down her cheeks. "What are you going to do?"

I glanced sideways at Sage who nodded encouragingly despite her reticence and worry for me.

"I've decided to donate."

"Oh."

Her hand shot to her face, covering her mouth, and then her shoulders shook violently, silent tears turning into racking sobs. I indicated for Sage to close the door. The last thing any of us needed was for Thomas to hear his mother's upset and come running before Helen and I had a chance to talk properly.

"Oh, Elliot. I'll never be able to thank you enough for saving my boy's life."

I held up my palm. "There's a long way to go yet, Helen." I didn't want to strip her happiness, but neither should she get ahead of herself. "A lot of hoops and hurdles to jump through and over. And I still have a gunshot wound to recover from."

Heat bloomed in her cheeks. "I understand."

I rubbed my fingertips over my lips. "Have you seen him?"

Sage, reading my stiff body language, pressed her leg closer to mine. I rested my hand on her thigh, signaling I was okay.

"Yes."

My jaw flexed, teeth grinding, bone on bone. "So you're standing by him then? After everything he's done."

She expelled a deep sigh, her hand absentmindedly running over the fabric of my couch, and she refused to look me straight in the eye.

"He's my husband, and despite everything he's done, I still love him, but no, Elliot. I'm not standing by him. I can forgive him for using his fists on me, but what he did to Athena, and to you, his own flesh and blood, who is to say he wouldn't do something like that to Thomas in the future? He lied to me, for years, and that kind of deception is hard to excuse."

"Does he know this?"

"Yes. I saw him two days ago and told him I was filing for divorce."

Tension clawed at my shoulders, and I rubbed the back of my neck. "Athena wants to see him."

"I know. She told me." She tilted her head to the side. "And given your expression, I'd guess you're not happy about it."

"No. But Athena is her own woman, and nothing I say will change her mind. If that's how she wants to get her closure, who am I to deny her?"

"When is she going?"

"We're both going on Thursday."

Before Helen could respond, Athena returned with a grinning Thomas.

I smiled and patted the seat beside me. "Got a little bit of chocolate ice cream there, buddy." I licked my thumb and rubbed his cheek.

"Elliot?"

"Yeah?"

"I always wanted a big brother."

My chest tightened, and instantly, I knew that by donating a kidney to this kid, my brother, I'd fill the hole inside me that until now, I hadn't known how to plug, instead cramming it with anger and hatred and loathing.

I ruffled his hair. "And now you have one."

Chapter Twenty-Nine

ELLIOT

I CUT THE ENGINE AND SHIFTED AROUND IN MY seat. Athena sat in the back of the car threading the remains of a ripped tissue through her hands. She glanced out the window at the imposing brick building, razor wire atop the eight-foot walls, and uncertainty flooded her face.

"Hey, you don't have to go in there. It doesn't matter that it's all arranged. He can go fuck himself."

"Absolutely," Sage interjected. "No one is putting any pressure on you, Athena."

A wry smile touched her lips, and she blew out a heavy sigh. "Except for myself. I just know that if I don't do this, I'll regret it."

I unclipped my belt and drew Sage in for a kiss. "Are you sure you're okay waiting here?"

She'd wanted to come to provide Athena with a female shoulder to cry on in case she needed it. However you looked at it, today was going to be a shit show. None of us, Athena especially, knew how she'd react to seeing a man she was too young to remember. Let alone reconciling that with knowing he'd snatched her off the streets of New York and kept her in a cold, damp, filthy basement, and chained to a pipe for more than twenty-four hours.

All in the name of money.

"Yes. I've brought a book, so I'll sit here in the quiet and read. Take your time."

I put my arm around Athena's shoulders as we crossed the parking lot toward the visitors' entrance. Every step made my skin crawl. I hated that my sister had to come to a place like this to get the answers she sought.

We completed the relevant entrance requirements and handed over all our personal items. The guards subjected both of us to a body scan to ensure we weren't bringing in contraband, and only then were we led into the main visitors' area.

There were ten booths, and a thick pane of glass separated us from the prisoners. We were told to sit in booth six and wait.

Once every booth had a visitor assigned, a buzzer sounded, and a door in the corner, on the other side of the glass, opened. Prisoners filed in, all dressed in identical jumpsuits.

Athena stiffened beside me, her eyes scanning the line of men. I felt around for her hand, clasping her fingers in an attempt at solidarity. She shot me a grateful smile.

"Thank you for coming with me. I know this is hard on you."

"It's not exactly a party for you, either," I said.

And then I saw him.

Seventh in line.

He locked gazes with me, mine filled with animosity, his

belligerent in his defiance. He plunked himself down on the metal chair and folded his arms.

"You survived, I see," he drawled.

"No thanks to you," I bit out.

He shrugged. "You shouldn't have come looking for me."

I snorted a bitter laugh. "And you shouldn't have kidnapped your own daughter. Aren't you even going to acknowledge her?"

"Elliot." Athena squeezed my hand.

He shifted in his seat and turned toward Athena. "You're so like your mother." He smiled, but it barely touched his cheeks. "She set all this in motion. She should have kept her damn mouth shut."

My free hand curled into a fist.

What I wouldn't give to smash it right into his face. I should have finished him off all those years ago when he came around begging for money, and then he wouldn't have taken Athena.

And Thomas wouldn't exist.

"Why did you take me?"

Athena's quiet voice, resonating with elegance and class, filled my chest with pride.

"If you needed money for Thomas's medical bills, then you should have just asked. None of this needed to happen."

He jabbed a finger in my direction. "I asked him for money once, and you know what I got? A broken fucking nose."

A smile edged across my face. "And if you weren't sitting behind that thick pane of glass, you'd have a busted jaw to go along with it."

He snorted, giving Athena his attention. "See? That's why. Besides, taking you was a lot more fun."

Anger propelled me from my chair, the metal legs scraping along the uneven floor. I slammed my fist on the small shelf in front of the glass.

"You'd better fucking hope you never get out of here, because if you do, I'll be waiting for you."

A guard dashed over and urged me to sit down or face eviction. Only the thought of leaving Athena here alone with that bastard, or stealing this chance to get closure away from her, sealed my mouth shut.

"All I want to know is would you have hurt me," Athena said. "One minute you said you wouldn't, and the next you threatened to cut off my fingers. Which was it?"

His bottom lip stuck out in a petulant pout. He let a few seconds scrape by, all the while picking at a scratch on the countertop.

"Empty threats," he eventually muttered. "Whadda you take me for?"

"We know the fucking answer to that," I snapped, shooting a hateful glare at the man whose DNA I shared. If I could cut out every fucking strand and burn them, I would.

"That's what I thought." Athena stood and smoothed the front of her skirt, then spun on her heel and walked off.

"Hey, wait."

I stood, too, pressing my fingertips onto the shelf I'd punched a few minutes ago. "She got what she came for."

I pivoted, intent on leaving like Athena had, but I'd only taken two steps when he called out.

"Don't you want to know how I did it?"

I hesitated, then slowly spun back around. "Did what?" I asked, although I suspected what he meant.

He rolled back his shoulders and ran his gaze over me, and in that moment, I saw the full evil of the man who'd brought me into this world reveal himself with sickening clarity.

"Evaded you for so long."

When I didn't reply, he continued.

"There are a lot of smart men in prison. For five years I had a cellmate, a financial genius. He talked. I paid attention. And you, with all your billions and rage and anger weren't smart enough to find me." He laughed. "It must kill you to know I outsmarted you."

It did, but I had no intention of ever letting this bastard know how torturous the last few years had been for me. Instead, I curled my lip, rested my fingertips on the countertop on my side of the thick pane of glass separating us, and smiled.

"And yet I'm the one who gets to walk out of here and go home to a family who loves me."

I pretended to leave once more, then turned back to face him for the last time.

"Oh, one more thing. I'm a match for Thomas, and yes, I will be donating a kidney to save *your* son. But not for you. For *me*." I poked myself. "Every time I look at that little boy, I'll smile, knowing that you'll never see him again. Once Helen divorces you, that's it. You're done. Thomas and Helen have a new family now. And what kind of future have you got, huh? Nothing except twenty-three hours a day locked in a cell. Because mark my words, I'll make sure you go down for a very long time."

He spluttered something else, but I didn't care to stick around to listen. I walked away, leaving behind the room that smelled of desperation, and the man who'd fathered us, tried to destroy us, but ultimately brought us even closer together.

———

Six Months Later...

"Elliot, put me down!" Sage demanded, pounding her fists on my ass where she dangled over my left shoulder.

I returned the favor, smacking her butt three times. "Quieten down, wench. We don't have long and I, for one, plan to enjoy every second between now and when our guests arrive."

We were hosting a party, and in about an hour, our family and friends would fill our new home overlooking Central Park. We had a lot to celebrate. I'd come through the transplant surgery with relatively few problems, Thomas's body hadn't rejected the kidney, although he wasn't totally out of the woods yet, Athena and Ryker were having another baby—a girl this time—and Sage's mom and sister had moved into a small house with a fenced-in yard less than fifteen minutes from us. One of the first things Sage had done was get a dog for her sister. Lily adored animals, and she and the one-year-old cute-as-a-button crossbreed Sage had rescued from the shelter were inseparable.

The other terrific piece of news I'd gotten this week had come from the courthouse. The judge had given that fucker a life sentence with parole only applicable after he'd served thirty-five years for kidnapping and extortion, and possession of a firearm which, as a convicted felon, he wasn't permitted to do. I fully expected him to die in prison, but if he made it out alive, he wouldn't be for long. I'd make sure of it.

We reached the top of the stairs, and I unceremoniously dropped her on the bed, then dove on top of her, tickling her without mercy. She squealed and pushed at my chest, but I was far too strong for her and she knew it. Her girlish giggles and harsh warnings of retribution when I least expected it filled my chest with a love I hadn't thought possible. For almost five years, the rabid need for revenge had consumed my life, but now that was behind us, the future ahead dazzled me with its brightness.

Forty-five minutes later, I reluctantly bowed to Sage's insistence that we get ready to greet our guests. If it were up to me, I'd have left it until the last minute if it meant I got to spend a bit more time devouring the woman I adored, but she seemed to think that hosting a party while smelling of sex wasn't appropriate.

We made it with about three and a half minutes to spare. Upton and Garen and their girlfriends were the first to arrive which, considering they had the farthest to travel—except for Sebastian, who was flying in from London—was a bit fucking rich. My parents arrived next, along with Sage's mom and Lily, and then Helen and Thomas. I bumped fists with my little brother, and he gave me the smile he kept only for me. After what we'd gone through together, we'd always share a special bond. Mom and Dad had welcomed Thomas and Helen into our family with open arms, and not for the first time, I realized how incredibly lucky I was to have such amazing parents. In the last few months since Athena and I visited *him* in prison, I'd hardly given him a second thought. When I'd given evidence at his trial, I'd refused to give him the satisfaction of even glancing in his direction. And the night the news of his sentence came through, I'd cracked open a particularly expensive bottle of bourbon and got roaring drunk.

Once the rest of our guests had arrived, and I'd made sure they all had drinks, I tapped a spoon on the side of my glass, and the room fell silent.

"Thanks for coming, everyone, especially you guys who had to travel a fair distance. Odd how you were the first to arrive." I stared pointedly at my sister. She giggled and snuggled into Ryker's side. "It's been a tough few years for me and my family, and I know I've been insufferable at times."

"Understatement of the century," Ryker coughed out, a barb he received a few chuckles for.

"You're lucky there are children present," I said. "Anyway, as I was saying before being rudely interrupted, it's been a bit rough, and yet despite it all, the people in this room are the ones who stuck by me through it all. Even tossing me out of ROGUES was for my own good, although it stung like hell at the time." I curved an arm around Sage's waist and drew her closer to me. "The start of this year looked to be just as crappy as the last, and then this gorgeous girl came back into my life, and from there on in, everything just clicked into place. I'm not sure what I did to deserve her, but I know that I'll never let her go."

I set down my glass on a nearby table and slipped my hand into my pocket. Dropping to one knee, I opened a black velvet box and held it out in front of me.

"Oh God," Sage mumbled.

"Not quite, but close." I grinned. "I mightn't have plucked up the courage to ask you to be mine sixteen years ago, but I won't make the same mistake twice. Sage Abbott, I love you and I can't think of a better place to ask you to marry me than right here, in our first home together, in front of all the people we love and who love us in return. I don't really know what I'll do if you say no, so please save me from Ryker's endless ribbing and say yes."

She clasped her hand to her chest, and then she dropped down onto her knees and kissed me. I vaguely heard the cheering, whooping, and hollering, but it came at me through a fog. There was only me and her, and a lifetime of happiness stretching out before us.

We broke apart, and I stared into her dove-grey eyes.

"Is that a yes?" I whispered.

"It's a yes today, tomorrow, and forever."

Two years ago, the perfect woman walked into my life —on the arm of my brother.

From the moment I saw Trinity Lane, I wanted her, but despite the absolute contempt I have for my brother, there's a code, one I won't break.

Not even the night she lands on my doorstep a quivering wreck and refuses to tell me a damn thing... Or when he comes looking for her with guilt in his eyes.

But sometimes our choices have a habit of exploding in our faces. None more so than the one I made by letting her walk away.

It's the last mistake I'll make. I'll shatter all the rules to keep her safe—and keep us both alive.

Acknowledgments

I am so very lucky to have the most amazing team of people around me, all of whom love and support me every step of the way.

Hubs - thank you for supporting me in following my dreams. I know it's not always easy, especially when my mind wanders when you're trying to talk to me. Your patience with how much my characters overtake me at times knows no bounds. Love you to bits.

To my critique partner, Incy... Thank you so much for your critique on this novel once again, and for helping me navigate this challenging story. I appreciate and love you so very much.

To my amazing, funny, kind, generous, wonderful PA, Loulou. I love that you love Elliot. I'll loan him to you at weekends - if only for the banter and sexual-innuendos!

Emmy - thank you for your terrific editing as always.

Katie - giiirrrllll! I love you and appreciate you so much, but none more so than the time you put into reading for me and picking up those blooming Britishisms that just insist on slipping through the net.

Jean - God, I can't wait to hug the life out of you in November! So happy you loved Elliot, and got to see more of your Ryker. So much love coming your way.

Jacqueline - Thank you for reading, as always. I appreciate you so very much. Looking forward to when we can meet up for a coffee - please let it be soon!

To my ARC readers. You guys are amazing! You're my final eyes and ears before my baby is released into the world and I appreciate each and every one of you for giving up your time to read.

And last but most certainly not least, to you, the readers. Thank you for being on this journey with me. It still humbles me to think that my words are being read all over the world.

If you have any time to spare, I'd be ever so grateful if you'd leave a short review on Amazon or Goodreads. Reviews not only help readers discover new books, but they also help authors reach new readers. You'd be doing a massive favor for this wonderful bookish community we're all a part of.

About Tracie Delaney

Tracie Delaney is an author of more than twenty-five contemporary romance novels which she writes from her office in the freezing cold North West of England. The office used to be a garage, but she needed somewhere quiet to write and so she stole it from her poor, long-suffering husband who is still in mourning that he's been driven out to the shed!

An avid reader for as long as she can remember, Tracie was also a bit of a tomboy back in the day and used to climb trees with her trusty Enid Blyton's and read for hours, returning home when it was almost dark with a numb bottom and more than a few splinters!

Tracie's books have a common theme of strong women who aren't afraid to go after what they want and alpha males who put up a great fight (which they ultimately lose!)

At night she likes to curl up on the sofa with her two Westies, Murphy & Cooper, and binge-watch shows on Netflix. There may be wine involved.

Visit her website at www.authortraciedelaney.com

Printed in Great Britain
by Amazon

46659519R00152